G. Doyle

PUFFIN BOOKS

Editor: Kaye Webb

FINN'S FOLLY

The car had gone away. There was nothing now, except mist in the hills ... and Max, Brenda, Tony and David (David who was different from other children) were left alone in the holiday shack at Lakeside, waiting for their parents to return.

The semi-trailer had pulled out of the city back-loaded with chemicals ... it went grinding through hills and valleys at a steady fifty on the flat. *Speed It Thru Mac*: that was the sign on top. Alison sat beside her father in the cabin, dozing ... until suddenly she jolted awake, pitched hard against her safety belt as the truck shuddered to a stop. 'Sorry, love,' her father said, 'I've got myself lost.'

Fog. A country road in Australia. A hairpin bend. These are the circumstances, this is the situation out of which Ivan Southall weaves his moment-by-moment narrative of a single night when five young people and five adults are involved in a drama of life — and death. To each of them, until that night, a road accident was something that happened to other people (you read about them, heard about them, every day of the week). But when Max, Brenda, Tony and David, Alison, and Frank and Phyllis Ashford find they are the actual players in the aftermath of tragedy instead of onlookers, then the real impact is made clear.

For readers of ten and over.

Cover design by Don Black

Ivan Southall

Finn's Folly

Penguin Books

in association with H. J. Ashton, Auckland and Sydney

Penguin Books Ltd, Harmondsworth,
Middlesex, England
Penguin Books Australia Ltd, Ringwood,
Victoria, Australia

First published by Angus and Robertson 1969
Published in Puffin Books 1972
Copyright © Ivan Southall, 1969

Printed in Australia for
Penguin Books Australia Ltd
at The Dominion Press,
Blackburn, Victoria

ONE

Shelter Near a Rock

THERE WASN'T MUCH about Lakeside that Max didn't know; every tree, every rock, every faintly worn track. He had had seven years to find out. He was fed up with Lakeside. Much the same went for Brenda and Tony. David was a different proposition.

Max was eight when his father had walked in one day trying not to grin. Dad could never keep a secret, not properly; his secrets always stuck out like a sore thumb. 'Tomorrow I'm taking you for a drive to show you something good. Perhaps we'll stay overnight and come back Sunday.' They had driven out of town at half-past six in the morning, Mum questioning him, again and again. 'What have you done?'

But Dad went on grinning for a hundred and eighty miles that never seemed to end, while for everyone else the joke wore thin. The children, except David, were quarrelsome and cross. ('When are we going to get there? I wanna go to the lav. How many more miles? How many have we done?') They were then a little too young for journeys that dragged on for hours.

'This is ridiculous,' Mum had said.

The car turned away from railway lines and highways, away from town and farms, and took a third-class road into mountains.

At a high place Dad had stopped. A reservoir lay below

like a mirror in the sun; a huge earth wall at one end, long tails of water at the other; miles of water flooding several valleys.

'I don't understand,' Mum had said.

'Down there. Do you see it? Near the water's edge.'

'See what?' Mum had said.

'The shack.'

'What shack? What have you done?'

'That shack,' Dad had said, 'the seventh past the jetty on the north arm of the lake. Isn't it like something that's right out of this world?'

'It's out of this world all right,' Mum had said. 'It's almost off the edge. Two hundred miles for *that*? What's so special about a shack?'

'I've leased it from the Water Commission. It's ours until the year 2001. For David,' Dad said. 'It'll help, don't you think?'

After seven years of holidays, seven years of occasional weekends, hours in the car to get there, hours in the car to get back, there was nothing about Lakeside that anyone could tell Max. But what it had meant to David could only be guessed.

It wasn't easy living with David; he complicated even simple things like meals, or bedtime, or study, or taking a walk. David came first; he was last in all things, but first.

That was what Mum said, her very words: 'Last in all things, but first.'

The door opened with a faint squeak and Mum was there. The squeak startled Max, although he had been expecting it to happen. For some reason the moment was not welcome.

A low, tired light from the kitchen end of the long living-room showed her standing there, a bulky shadow enlarged by a heavy coat, a shapeless felt hat, and a thick scarf at her neck. It didn't look like Mum at all. 'Are you awake?' she asked quietly.

Max raised himself on an elbow and felt the cold strike down into the disturbed bed. He had the strangest feeling that something about this moment was important. It had a *hidden* importance, as when you detected a deliberate step in someone's stride, or heard the theme tune that announced the national news.

'It's nearly twelve-thirty,' Mum said. 'Are you sure you'll be all right?'

He nodded.

'I'll be back by two. It looks like a mist up in the hills, but I'll hurry if I can. I suppose I could be another quarter-hour.'

'I don't want you to hurry, Mum. Why should you?'

She crossed the room to Tony's bed and tucked him in, unnecessarily, because Tony slept like a log of wood. 'He's asleep,' she whispered, 'so's Brenda, but I'm not sure about David.' Mum seemed to be undecided. 'I don't like leaving you until David settles.'

'I can cope, Mum. You'll have Dad waiting in the cold.'

He could see that she was impatient to get away, that she was on edge, as she often was when Dad wasn't around.

'If you do hear David,' she said, 'it'll probably be for the lav. I suppose I should have got him out an hour ago, but I dozed off, and flattened the lights; your father *will* be pleased; but it's such a long wait until half-past twelve. Make sure you snib David's door when you take him back to his room. I don't want him wandering round in the dark. The way you all sleep he'd be gone before you knew.'

'I'll make sure, Mum.'

'The fire's out and everything's locked up. There's nothing to worry about.'

'Of course there isn't. I'm not worried, Mum. I'm fifteen, not nine or ten.'

'I'm still prepared to take you all with me.' Was it that Mum had a guilty conscience or was it her habit of making difficulties for herself? The problems Mum thought up were a family joke. 'I don't mind at all, Max, if I have to. I've always done it before.'

'I'm not the least worried, Mum, honest I'm not. I'm grown up now. There's nothing round here that could hurt a fly. Specially this week.'

She might have smiled, but he wasn't sure. 'I must admit

it's a drag with a car-load of cross children. Tony's so
tiresome when he's woken up.' She kissed his cheek. 'We'll
try not to disturb you when we come in.'

The door faintly squeaked again as it closed, and darkness
came back. In a few moments Max heard the click of the
outside lock and Mum's heels on the steep wooden ramp,
slipping a bit, perhaps on frost. It was a relief, in a way, to
hear her go; not to have to talk any more. It was an awful
effort talking when you were half-asleep. He eased back
into the bed to get away from the cold.

The car, down below, began to murmur through the
house, throbbing in the floorboards, making things vibrate
as it always did. It was a sleek English car with automatic
transmission, reluctant to pull away smoothly before the
engine was hot. Warming-up was a drill that Dad insisted
upon. It buzzed down there in the excavation between the
foundations like bees swarming. It was a terrific car even
though it was eight years old.

'It's a real machine,' Dad often said, to the point of boring
everyone, 'engineered like the Lancaster I flew as a lad.'
Dad got a lot of pleasure from sitting behind the wheel,
especially while the engine warmed up. He presided over
the gleaming instrument panel of real wood and real
instruments like the pilot he used to be when there was a
war on and he was young. 'This business of a new car every
twelve months,' he often said, 'from the end of an assembly
line, miles long, is all right for some, but not for me.'

The car was gone. (Mum's warm-up took less time than
Dad's.) That characteristic note, part snarl, part hum, was
moving about as though transported into the sky. It was
on the high road, hugging the curves, with thirty-two miles
ahead of it across the hills and over the plain to Hamer.
The night train stopped there at twenty minutes past one.

Max was master of the house—unless Brenda woke up!
It was a disquieting feeling, even though he had assured
Mum it was not.

But the fire was out, the doors were locked, the windows
were bolted, Brenda and Tony were asleep, David seemed
to be all right, and the forest was breathlessly still with

frost crystallizing on leaves, birds silent, frogs silent, even insects insensible from cold.

He became a part of that world outside, stiffening with it into immobility. Blood in the veins of animals flowed slower, sap in trees sank back into the roots, breezes froze solid far away, the lake was like plate-glass feet thick, even the outlet from the dam, miles downstream, heard thundering into the aqueduct when the wind blew from that quarter, gave up no sound.

Silence was poised as though balanced on a blade at the brink of a pit.

Max shivered.

The car had gone away. Perhaps he heard it blare on the hairpin bend, perhaps not. Both Mum and Dad were child-like on that bend, burbled into it, blared out of it, giving the pedal the gun.

There was nothing now, except mist in the hills, if Mum had spoken right. Had mist swallowed her up? He strained his ears until they ached, but nothing was there except a hollow beat inside his own head.

Alison had never become accustomed to it. Something about her must have been made wrong. She was sick inside from being jolted, half-stupefied from tiredness and noise, couldn't stay properly awake, couldn't fall mercifully asleep. It was never any different. She hated driving in the truck by night. But she would never have breathed a hint of her dislike to Dad.

How on earth he could sit at that wheel with a straight back and remain alert defeated her understanding. He stopped at roadhouses for cups of coffee and steak and eggs, but the pep pills that transport drivers were said to take were no part of Dad's make-up. Dad did it out of the strength that was in himself.

He was proud of his strength; perhaps even vain about it; still cut a firm figure (and knew it) stripped for the beach; still looked young, although Alison knew he was forty-three. There wasn't much about him she didn't know; he had been both father and mother to her for so long. But

Dad drove himself hard too. 'Got to, love,' he said, 'the only way we'll get rich is earn it myself.'

He had pulled out of the city back-loaded with chemicals at about eight o'clock, then had driven west, heading for home, grinding through hills and valleys and at a steady fifty on the flat. Something about him seemed inhuman. He drove with his jaw set, his lean, hard body upright, his arms extended like branches of trees. To sense him there at any time was to shelter near a rock; to be far away from him at school was to feel somehow incomplete.

'You're a dad's girl,' the kids said, 'but who'd blame you with a smasher for a dad like that?' They didn't know he drove a truck; it was hard to say whether it would have mattered or not. 'Don't you tell those kids,' Dad said, 'let 'em think you're Lady Muck.' The headmistress knew, but kept it to herself, solemnly, as she would a state secret. Mr McPhee was in the 'transport' industry, interstate. The kids didn't know that his business was a one-man show, that his industry was his own sweat, that his 'plant' was a solitary semi-trailer with a sign on top in red and white paint: SPEED IT THRU MAC.

He didn't work at weekends as a general thing; but kept them free for Alison. But term holidays were different; they were together then all the time. 'Where'd you go during the holidays?' the kids always asked. 'Sydney,' Alison would say (or Brisbane or Melbourne or Canberra or Broken Hill), 'Dad had business there and he took me along.' 'You're lucky,' the kids always said, 'having a father who's a friend. Ours go alone. They never take us.'

She jolted awake, pitched hard against her safety belt. Dad was muttering to himself. The transport shuddered to a stop almost in the trees (trees like piles seen beneath the surface of a pond), and Dad was limp at the wheel as though his ramrod back had snapped, 'Sorry, love,' he said, 'I've got myself lost.'

She felt sick, but not from fright, and peered out into fog. That was why the trees had looked odd. Then she looked for the road but could see only a track.

'Lost?' she said. 'Where?'

'On the way to Uncle Fred's.'

'Who's Uncle Fred?'

'Fred, love. You know Fred. No, maybe you don't. He's not your kind of bloke. I thought we'd pull in there for the night to get out of the fog. I'd swear I turned off on to the right track.'

He switched off the engine and lit a cigarette.

'What about the map?' she said.

'Maps are no good when you're lost. Sorry, love. But I don't like heading on into this. I don't know the road. There's nowhere to turn and the country's getting steep. If I try to swing her here, to back-track, I'll end up in the rough. That's something I don't fancy with a load like ours on the back.'

'Can't you recognize the country, Dad?'

'If I could, love, I wouldn't be lost. I need my head read for leaving the Highway. I'm nuts. I should have pulled in at Hamer and knocked them up at the pub.' He appeared to be extremely annoyed with himself. 'It's my own fault, penny-pinching again. I don't suppose Fred would have welcomed me, no matter what he says. "When are you going to drop in?" he always asks. Maybe friendship wouldn't stand the shock at a quarter to one on a foggy night.' He took a rug from the seat and tucked it round his legs. 'But maybe she'll clear in an hour or two. Who can tell? Curl up, love. Go back to sleep while the cabin's warm. She'll be colder than charity when that fog starts seeping in.'

He dimmed the lights. 'I'd swear it was the right track. "Twenty-three and three-tenth miles," Fred told me. "Exact. You can't miss. Finn's Folly, plastered up on a lump of tin. Dirty great mountains to the right of you, dirty great mountains to the left, Freddie Finn in the middle." That's what he said. But I've got the wrong track. On a night like this I pick a wrong-un. I'm nuts. When I think of that lovely warm bed at the pub . . .'

Alison nodded off. The things that Dad said didn't matter much. It was easy to sleep now that movement had stopped. When she woke again, in scarcely a minute it seemed, the door was open wide and Dad was yelling outside, 'Hey. Stop. *Stop*!'

There were headlights in the fog, coming downhill.

'Hey! Hey! Hey!'

The headlights went by.

Dad came back, stamping his feet more vigorously than he should have done if keeping them warm was his sole intent. 'Woman driver,' he said, 'confound my luck. I don't suppose you could expect a woman to stop.' He climbed back into the cab and slammed the door with a blast of icy air. 'It's cold out there, love, by George it is. Just as well we were off the road. If we'd struck her on a curve in a fog like this we'd have hit head-on.'

He started the engine and Alison sat upright.

'Are you going on, Dad?'

'I am, I am.'

'Is it wise?'

He laughed. 'Why not? The road can't be that bad, love. The woman was moving at a healthy rate of knots. She knew she was safe. Except for transports you don't expect! We can't stop here. We'll bally well freeze to death.'

He crept back on to the crown of the track, wheels spinning a bit on wet grass.

'She had to come from somewhere; maybe a town. Keep your eyes peeled. Look out for signposts and gateposts and tracks leading off. Maybe Fred can't count his miles. We mightn't have reached him yet.'

Alison wasn't really worried. To know that Dad was there was to shelter near a rock.

TWO

End of Term

MAX CURLED into a ball in the hollow of his bed, set about by air that was cold as ice, silent as space. Not only was he master of the house, but now, it seemed, he was the one and only crew member of a satellite orbiting the earth. It was the queerest feeling, completely new to him, in a way empty, in another way full, like a pain rushing in circles without a place to hurt in.

He couldn't stand the silence; perhaps for the first time in his life he had really noticed it. It wasn't natural, it wasn't right, and he tried to invent sounds to humanize it; with a terrific effort of will he wrestled in his mind to unseat an empty power kerosene drum from the shelf near the lighting plant under the house, just for the joy of listening to the crash. Comic book characters of a certain breed could move mountains by wishing, but that drum, empty or not, wouldn't budge an inch.

He was *wide* awake, with a cold nose and cold feet, a dribble from his nose and a dullness in his feet. He sniffed repeatedly and drew his feet up until his knees were under his chin. It was silly, but he was beginning to shiver for reasons other than cold. He didn't feel secure any more and couldn't work out why.

There was always noise at home in the city—perhaps that was it? Even in the dead hours something always stirred; there would be an ambulance wailing, milk bottles clinking, cats spitting, tyres squealing, babies crying. You always knew that life was there, a few feet away. But here there was nothing, no dogs barking, or traffic; nothing like that until tomorrow, until Mr and Mrs Logan arrived at the shack next door in their thumping great station-wagon with their thumping great Labradors that terrified David to tears. The Logans turned up full of hearty noises and good cheer almost every Saturday all the year round, sometimes with grandchildren, sometimes not.

There weren't any voices either; none that could be imagined at this hour of the night. The Fenwicks were too far round the lake, next to the jetty, a mile at least, and were probably in bed. The Fenwicks had no kids, anyway. The Fenwicks 'had each other', as they liked to explain at length to the grown-ups (kids never seemed to count with the Fenwicks), but even they were not likely to talk while they were asleep. Though maybe they did! Max, a little guiltily, imagined that he was projecting his ears like great feelers round the lake between the trees to stick them like a stethoscope to the wall of the Fenwicks' shack. It was so real that it made his ears *ache*. But there was not a sound, not a whisper. The Fenwicks worked for television and had tickets on themselves as big as roadside hoardings. Mrs Fenwick did loads of commercials with a soft, ingratiating voice and looked the camera in the eye as though it was her best friend and called everything marvellous and wonderful and beautiful and used the words 'sincerely recommend' an awful lot.

The Harleys and the Scotts had not turned up either, the creeps, although they had said they would, and all the other shacks along the shore were empty, blinds drawn, shutters closed, all desolate with ribbons of stringy bark lying over their roofs like torn shirt sleeves and spider webs in horrible dirty grey tangles under the eaves. No one with any brains ever came to Lakeside in winter. The Fenwicks came only to strike a pose: 'Our retreat from the rat-race,' they called it, 'to get away from jangling telephones and the madding crowd.' A statement made public in an article about them in a TV magazine. The Logans came only from force of habit, because they were old and couldn't break the habit. The Shaws came because of David.

'It's too cold up there in August,' Max had said to Mum weeks before the school term had ended. 'Golly, Mum, it's deadly. We're *slaves* to habit. Do we have to go again this year for the whole ten days? Dad can't get away from work till the weekend and you know how he hates travelling on the train. Poor old Dad, sitting in that train for hours and hours. Sufferin'. Can't we stay at home instead? Can't we see some shows in town or something? Even the *zoo*. It always rains up there. Last year we had sleet.'

Mum had been impatient. 'You should be old enough to appreciate it.'

'I'll bet you here and now the Harleys don't turn up, or the Scotts either.'

'Oh, Max. When they *are* there you're squabbling all the time. And we're not like the Scotts or the Harleys; it's different. We've *got* to have a change of scene. That's why your father signed the lease. He knew that I had to get out of these walls with David. In this thing you've got to pull your weight. You and Tony and Brenda have everything; David has nothing. He looks forward to the lake so much.'

'He doesn't look forward to it. He doesn't know the difference.'

'I'll have no more of that!'

It was a dead-end. It was no use arguing. David came first. And just because David never talked except for baby stuff, or did anything much except wreck the place, did it mean that he was without feeling? You never knew what David was thinking. You never knew whether he could think at all, for David was different.

'How did it happen, Mum?' Max had asked, only the once. He had never been brash enough to ask again.

Mum had floundered at first. It was a question she had not expected from Max. Perhaps she had thought he would understand without being told. But he didn't understand, and understood less because that crumb Leo Cootes had said, 'Is your brother an idiot?'

'Of course not!' Max's hair had bristled. He had felt it

stand up on the back of his neck. 'Strike me, Leo; that's a horrible word.'

'Well, what is he then?'

'Mentally retarded; I guess.'

Leo hadn't thought much of that. 'Strewth. That's what me mum calls me when she's doin' a rave, but I'm not like *him*.'

So Max had asked, 'Please, Mum, how did it happen?'

'I don't know, and even if I did, what difference would it make?' For a moment it had seemed she was going to walk away, as she sometimes did when difficult questions popped up. 'Knowing how and why these children are born interests doctors and scientists a great deal. They're full of bright ideas. But for families who have the problem it's not an academic question.'

She had looked a bit weepy then. 'Nature made a mistake when David was born. Knowing why there was a mistake will never unmake the mistake. The child born his way stays that way. It's not sickness; it's not insanity; it's *difference*. Nothing done by us, as far as anyone knows, could have caused it or prevented it. You don't have bad blood in your veins, if that's what troubles you. Nothing about us Shaws need make you ashamed. This is not to say that everyone understands, because everyone doesn't. It's not that people are vicious; it's simply that they're ignorant.'

She had run out of breath. 'David is different,' she went on after a pause. 'I don't know what goes on inside him, because I can't speak with him. I can't converse with my son. He can't be educated as you are; can't be taught more than the simplest things. He will exist, as far as I know, a short distance away from the world we live in until the day he dies. So close to us, but not quite with us. Every child like David is the innocent victim of what we call chance. One extra chromosome; forty-seven instead of forty-six. It could have been you. It could have been Leo Cootes. It could have been anyone. Some people call it an act of God; but I doubt if God whoops for the joy of it any more than I do.'

Perhaps Max had caught his mother unawares or trapped her into saying things she would rather not have said. He used to wonder sometimes what David would have been like if the 'mistake' hadn't happened. It was a waste of emotion.

He sat up in bed, shivering from head to foot, beset by miseries, irritated by Tony's deep, untroubled breathing. Imperturbable Tony. Tony the Tortoise, the kids called him. He sounded like a fat cat curled up on a cushion.

Max groped in the dark for his socks and roll-neck sweater, then padded out into the living-room, feeling his way, curling his toes under to protect them from stubbing on chair legs and obstacles. He hated stubbing his toes and if it had happened just then he would burst into tears, a most unmanly state of affairs. The torch was not in its place— Mum must have taken it—so he fumbled on farther to the light switch, but need not have bothered. The light was a pale yellow glimmer, as Mum had said. The storage batteries after a punishing week were flattened—a job for Dad first thing in the morning, starting up the engine. Recharging the batteries was Dad's job because the cranky old engine packed a backfire like a kick in the stomach.

Mum had said the fire was out, and how right she was. There was nothing but a heap of ashes stained with black dribbles of water. Anything less cheerful than a living-room without people at one o'clock in the morning he could not imagine; a living-room lined with doors, like panels, and beyond, silence.

He took a rug from the settee, draped it like a cloak from his shoulders and stood on the hearth mat, swaying.

'*Bust it.*'

He started pacing in an irritable, ridiculous circle, round and round the rug. 'Mum should've just upped and gone. It was all settled. What the blazes did she wake me up for?'

He was making himself giddy, so reversed his circle then suddenly abandoned it, to rip apart the curtains that screened the night from him. He couldn't see a thing until he rubbed clear a peephole in the misted window. There was moonlight but the moon was out of his vision. There lay the lake, motionless; no lights, no people, nothing outside but a world freezing over, and inside a weary lamp becoming dimmer. There was about this night a feeling that he wished had never happened.

A movement startled him, much more than it normally would have done. It was Brenda, in her nightdress, shivering. Brenda had long yellowish hair that fell to her shoulders, and freckles (to her sorrow) that made her face look dirty. The whites of her eyes seemed luminous. 'Mum gone?' she said.

'Blow you,' he said, 'you scared me to death. Yeh, mum's gone.'

'Gone long?'

'Half an hour. What are you doing out of bed?'

'Same as you, I suppose. Can't sleep. Must have been the car or you floundering round out here like a blooming elephant.' Brenda couldn't stop shivering. She thought Max looked ridiculous, the long, skinny streak, with his legs like broomsticks poking out from underneath.

'What'd you let the fire go out for?' she asked.

'I didn't. Mum put it out.'

'Well, we're not practising to be Eskimos, are we? Light the radiator, why don't you?'

'Crikey, sis. It's the middle of the night. You don't light radiators in the middle of the night.'

'I can't think of a better time to light them. You're so *dull*, Max. Standing there shivering.'

'I'm not shivering.'

'Be a sport, Max. Put a match to it. There's plenty of gas for it. Lighting things like that is man's work. Mum wouldn't expect us to shiver.'

'She'd expect us to be in bed.'

'Well, we're not. Go on, light it. I'll put on something warm.'

Arguing with Brenda was a waste of time. 'A born woman,' Dad said of her. 'Our first female Prime Minister in the making, mark my word.'

'Light a candle, too,' she called from her room, 'before

the batteries are flatter than a tack. Dad'll kill you if he has to crank it by hand.'

'Strike me,' Max moaned, 'she'll have them all awake. *Shut up, will you!*'

Brenda came back tying the cord of her dressing-gown. She looked more than ever almost a full-grown woman. Take away her freckles, add a couple of inches, slap on a bit of paint, and she'd pass for an eighteen-year-old. At fourteen she was bossier than an eighteen-year-old already. Worse than cousin Jenny.

'We'll have tea,' she said, 'and toast with honey.'

'You can make it,' Max said sullenly.

'You don't think I'd let *you* make it, do you? I don't want it burnt to a cinder.' She headed for the kitchen end of the room in the brightening flicker of the candle flame. 'Turn that switch off, Max. What's the use of a candle if you leave the light burning? Dad'll kill you. You know what he's like when he's got to crank that engine.'

'Yeh, yeh; I heard you before. Give your voice a rest. will you? You'll wake up David.'

'What time did Mum say she'd be back?'

'Depends on the train.'

'We're almost out of bread. I wonder if Mum knows? We'd better skip the toast or we'll have none for breakfast. What about coffee instead of tea?'

'Whatever you say. I don't care. Just be quiet, sis, *please*.'

Brenda leant on the counter top and cupped her chin in her hands. 'Funny, isn't it? The middle of the night. Just the gas hissing and things. I don't think I've been up at one o'clock before. I thought you'd be tired in the middle of the night. I'm not tired the least little bit.'

Max groaned. 'You didn't have to tell me that. You're like a brass band.'

'Is there a frost outside?'

'Yeh.'

'Mist up top?'

'Yeh.'

'I hope Mum doesn't skid on the road.'

'You're too much for me,' Max said, 'I'm going back to bed.'

'Don't go, Max.' Her voice had changed.

He squinted at her. 'Why?'

'I don't know.'

Something in Max responded to her tone and he sank back into the settee, confused, waiting developments, but nothing happened except that his feeling of insecurity was worse than before. 'You've been up at one o'clock often,' he said.

'Have I?'

'Yeh.'

'Tell me when?'

'I don't know when. Does it matter?'

'Of course it does. You can't say a thing like that without a reason.'

'Golly, sis, don't let's fight about it.'

'I'm not fighting. Who brought it up? I'm asking a question. Come on, tell me when I've been up at one o'clock before.'

He groaned, bewildered as always by Brenda's readiness to pick a squabble. 'Forget it, forget it, why don't you? Does it matter? I was only making talk.'

'Well don't, if you can't say anything sensible.'

'For cryin' out loud, sis. You're the one that asked me to stay. Blow you. I'm goin' to bed.' But he didn't make a move to get up, not even inwardly. 'Look, sis,' he said, 'what did you ask me to stay for?'

She gestured limply with her hands. 'I heard the car warming up. I listened to it go away. That's all.'

'You asked me to stay because of *that*?'

She busied herself with the coffee jar and didn't look up. 'You know what I mean,' she said awkwardly, 'or you wouldn't be out here yourself.'

'I *don't* know what you mean.'

She glanced at him suddenly, almost furtively. 'You do, but you're too miserable to say it. You wouldn't agree with me to save your life.'

Max shifted uncomfortably because for once Brenda's words were true; true and not to be answered; never, never to be agreed with. It was bad enough knowing that somehow or other she had tuned in on his wavelength.

THREE

Where Stillness Began

ALISON SAW THE signpost coming up before her father spotted the fork in the road. The transport's progress was laborious.

'There, Dad,' she said sharply.

He jabbed almost nervily at the brake pedal.

'Good, good. Can you read it?'

'No.'

His grunt was half-sigh and he applied the handbrake to assist his foot pressure. It was a big vehicle and a deceptively steep slope. The headlights shone into timber, into trees that looked like ghosts; a flood of light diffused by fog and further diffused by the windscreen constantly misting over.

'Can you see it now?'

'No, Dad. It's washed-out. Old, I guess.'

'Let's hope the blamed thing's not so old as to be unreadable.'

There was a thin quality about his voice that she had heard only rarely, each occasion so long ago it was astonishing she remembered it. Or was her 'remembering' nothing but fancy? Once when he had had to tell her that her mother had 'gone away' and would not be back, and later when he had left her at boarding school for the first time of her life. With the thinness his diction became coarse.

'Hop out,' he said, 'and have a look. Be careful, love. The steps'll be slippery.'

It was like stepping into a freezer, but less foggy than she had thought. It was the cab that made it seem worse, the misting up, the smear of the windscreen wipers.

'Do you want the torch?'

'No, Dad.'

The road was sticky beneath her feet, glazed with red mud (she thought it was red, and shuddered, as red as blood), and the air was sharp with pungent diesel fumes pouring from the exhaust into the fog. Lying beyond the note of the engine was a disturbingly deep stillness, as though the world had shrunk to the limits defined by the lights. Only a fool would venture beyond the lights. There was nothing out there where the stillness began.

It was a signpost with three arms. To Hamer, back down the road along which they had come, 27 miles; to Lookout, 3 miles; to Lakeside, 5. It was old, faded, leaning, and not as firm in the ground as it should have been. She gave it a wobble, then headed back for the warmth of the cab and thankfully shut the door on the night. She was shivering intensely and felt sore in the stomach.

'Well?'

'Hamer 27. Lookout 3. Lakeside 5.'

'*Lakeside!* Where the devil's that?'

Alison had no opinion.

'Which way?'

'To the right.'

'You're sure? The post was loose.'

'The third arm pointed back to Hamer, Dad; so the others must have been right.'

'O.K.,' he said, 'I suppose that makes sense. Pull out the map, love.'

'Can't you turn on the fork? Wouldn't it be better to go back?'

'I'm not turning here, not on your life. We'd be over the edge. If we had wings we could take off into space with a running jump.'

His finger tips drummed the wheel. He looked a different sort of man.

'Dad, do you think we ought to stop here?'

'I'm nuts,' he said, not hearing her. 'But what else could I have done? I *had* to keep going once I'd started. I've got to find somewhere to turn. Blast the fog.'

It was not like Dad to swear or to involve her in his anxieties.

'How am I going to get out of this place?'

'Dad,' she said, 'stop here. I'm not worried about the cold. You don't have to keep going because of me. Please!'

His voice dropped suddenly to a lower but harder level. 'What about the map, love?'

She spread it on the seat where he could see it, but he started wiping the windscreen with a cloth. 'Leave me out of it,' he said, 'you're navigator for tonight. My job's the road. Find Lakeside for me. Tell me where it is.'

'I can't, Dad.' She almost was afraid to say it. 'There's nothing near Hamer with a name like that.'

'There must be.'

'There isn't.'

'No road even?'

'Not on the map. Really there isn't. I suppose the scale's too small. It's only a track. Maybe it's not important enough to put on the map.'

'All right, love; I believe you; don't flap.'

'There's a dam.'

'Is there? Got a name on it?'

'Nothing. Only *Dam*. Nothing else.'

'That's got to be it, then, hasn't it? Lakeside's got to be a park beside the dam or something of the sort. That woman in the car came from somewhere. It'd be odd if she came from Fred's.'

'The Lookout's closer. Perhaps she came from there.'

'If she did it's our bad luck. I'm not aiming to get stuck on a mountain top. This is no Mini we're pushing love. We don't turn these things on a threepenny bit. Belt, love! Buckle it up.'

The headlights swung across foliage and the high fronds of ferns, bluntly, like searchlight cones on clouds, that she had seen in old television films about London in the war.

It was a trick of the fog, but the transport seemed to grope giddily into the air, not along the ground.

Then the lights came down out of the turn and rolled like masses of smoke on to the road ahead. It made her head spin. The way to Lakeside appeared to be downhill, but the hands of the clock surprised her more; green hands gleaming in the dark; they stood at twenty-five minutes to two. Thereafter she pretended to watch the clock because she was frightened to look out front. She glanced at Dad from the corners of her eyes.

There he sat as he had sat before, back straight (was it a pose?) arms like boughs of trees, but different. His voice was thin. His manner was coarse. Words uttered by him were not the words he had thought. All she had seen of him in fourteen years was a mask. ('Daddy, lift me up to touch the moon.' 'It's yours, love, from Daddy to you. But you mustn't touch or it might fall down.')

It was not his gentle lies that troubled her now. It was not his fear, because even heroes were afraid; she had learnt that from books. Other things had happened to reduce him to the level of ordinary men. Grown-up men who should know better. Men who swore under their breath when clean words would do. Men who spilt cigarette ash on their clothes and spat tobacco carelessly from the tips of their tongues. Men who said, 'Don't tell the kids at school I'm a truckie. Let them think you're Lady Muck.' Men of forty-three who fancied themselves on beaches. Men who said, 'Fred, love. You know Fred. No, maybe you don't. He's not your kind of bloke.' Why wasn't he her kind of 'bloke'?

Something inside Alison began to hurt. It was odd that thoughts like that should come into her head at a quarter to two in the morning. She hated them but couldn't drive them out.

Then Dad stopped again, foot on the brake. 'Lord, love,' he said, 'hairpin bend. Didn't you see it on the map?'

'No, I didn't,' she said, with unexpected heat, 'I'd have told you if I had.'

There was surprise in his voice. 'Hairpin bend, love. Hairpin bend!'

'I said it wasn't on the map. The road's not *on* the map.'

'All right, then, it's not, but it doesn't alter the fact. We can't go on and we can't back up. We're stuck.'

In a way, she could have cried. 'I'm sorry . . . I didn't mean to snap . . .'

He said nothing to that, but reached for a cigarette. 'Just my luck.' *Luck* came out gutturally, with a spit, but she knew he couldn't have said it any other way; the word had to sound like that even when she said it herself.

He reached for the handbrake, dimmed the lights, switched off the engine, but left the vehicle in gear. 'I'll have the torch, love,' he said.

'Are you going to chock the wheels?'

'I want to see what's out there. I've got to move somehow. I can't leave it here.'

'Please, Dad,' she said, 'don't move it. I'm scared.'

He laughed.

'Dad, it's going on for two.'

'Time's got nothing to do with it, love. We're a hazard to traffic.'

'Traffic, out here?'

'Just because the road's not on the map doesn't mean it's not used. And people who know the road may travel fast, too fast to stop for a truck they don't expect to meet.'

He went down over the side out into the fog and she heard him splutter from the cold.

'Dad,' she called fretfully, 'you said you couldn't go on and you couldn't back up. You said you were stuck. Why do you want to change your mind?'

His head appeared in the opening of the door. 'Look, love. It's not what a man says, it's what he does. A man's tongue wags in the middle—a bit like yours.'

Max and Brenda heard the car coming. Oh, it was a sound like laughter after a long, bad day.

They heard it up high somewhere, on the hill, on the straight stretch of road above the hairpin bend, and their eyes wider than usual looked directly into each other, each glimpsing something never suspected before, each realizing that some things between brother and sister were better without words.

The sound came through the gullies as the voices of children, skylarking at the bend, were sometimes tapped and relayed downward, yet when those same children moved fifty yards one way or another their voices could not be heard. Cars blaring into the hairpin bend and out of it passed through the same narrow belt. Still air or north wind brought down the sound.

It was there all right, it was true, the burble of an engine, its note rising and falling.

Brenda looked away from Max, suddenly embarrassed by his eyes. She even giggled a little. 'So much for my twinges,' she said, trying to joke her way out of a difficult moment. 'I guess I'll never get a job as a fortune-teller. In future I think I'll stick to maths.'

Max didn't quite know what to do with himself. He had never felt so thoroughly at sixes and sevens before, even rather light in the head. 'I don't know,' he said, 'how could a fellow have fastened on to a ratbag idea like that?' It was all right now to admit it out loud; it was all kinds of relief to admit it. The strain had been awful, parrying round the fear that something was going to happen, and drinking cup after cup of coffee to cover up. Looking back on it, as he suddenly did, he could scarcely believe he had been a part of it.

'Strike me, sis,' he said, 'I was sure. I was so blooming sure.'

'Of what?' she taunted.

'Oh, shut up.'

Then he saw the cups and the spoons and the spilt sugar and the condensed milk tin dribbling and the crumbs of biscuits. 'The place is a shambles. The mess you make. We'd better have a quick whip round and get back to bed. Though I'm blowed if I know how I'm going to sleep with all this coffee in me.' He darted for the radiator to turn it off.

'Look,' said Brenda, 'we can't tidy up in time; we haven't

a hope. Why hide the obvious? We'll have supper ready and surprise them.'

'Like fun we will. You know Mum. She'll scream, "Out of bed!" Natter, natter, natter. Not for this fellow, thank you very much. How would we explain? What would we say? She'd never leave us alone again.'

'Gee, you get over things quick.'

'It's got nothing to do with getting over anything. Come on, give us a hand.' He was blowing crumbs to the floor but looking up caught her frown, and that frown took him straight back several minutes through time. Incredibly, the sound of the engine was still there. 'Hey,' he said uneasily, 'they're still at the bend.'

'They are, too. I wonder why?'

They listened, and then Brenda said, 'Something's wrong. The car sounds odd.'

It sounded as it had never sounded, not since the day it had come home to the Shaws, but Max heard himself say, 'Can't be too much wrong. They've done the trip in an hour and twenty minutes. They have, you know. Sixty-four miles in eighty minutes. Whooh! And with a wait for a train in the middle.'

Brenda grasped at the thought, 'Yeh,' she said, 'you know Dad.' But she didn't believe herself and lapsed into silence. The same silence seemed suddenly to engulf the engine.

'They've moved, sis. They're coming.'

'They're not.'

'They are. Of course they are.'

'He's switched off, and you bloomin' well know he has.'

'Are you crackers, sis? We couldn't have heard the engine at any stage if it was only idling.'

'I don't care what you say. He's switched off. There's trouble.'

'So what? Even if he has. Maybe there's a tree down.' But something inside him sank into a hollow and he went to the window and rubbed a clear circle, hoping to discover heaven alone knew what. He peered out, hands like blinkers to his eyes. 'Hey,' he said. 'I can't see. It's fog. You can't see the water.'

'I told you, didn't I?' Brenda said.

'You told me what?'

She came over to the window and deliberately rubbed a circle for herself. 'Fog,' she said, 'you didn't say there was fog. What's wrong with you? How could it be Mum and Dad? How could they get back in that sort of time if there was fog?'

The injustice of her words and attitude angered him.

'It wasn't there before. And why blame me? You've got eyes of your own. Not an hour ago. It wasn't there then. I don't make the weather.'

'Well, if it's not Mum and Dad, who is it?'

'How the heck should I know? And who says it's not? Maybe they just ran into the fog, wham, and had to stop.'

'For a boy who's supposed to have brains you're plain wet. It wasn't our car and you know it. You're only kidding yourself. How could it have been, making a crummy noise like that?'

'You thought it was.'

'I did not. I thought it was a truck.'

'Who says it's a truck?'

'I do. With thieves in it, or someone, come to rob the shacks. Or convicts on the run. Or the army or—or anything. Maybe it's a tank.' Then Brenda started crying. 'It's not Mum, is it?'

Max groaned, half-bewildered, half-sympathetic. 'Of course it isn't. Not with the fog. She couldn't be back. She hasn't had time to get back. I wish you'd shut up snivelling or they'll *all* be awake.'

'I'm going to have a cup of coffee.'

'*Another one!* You'll blow up.'

'Gee, Max,' she said, 'I've never felt like this in my whole life and you're not much help.'

'Never felt like *what*?'

Then she really cried, and frightened him, and he put an arm around her because he knew he had to. Blood was thicker than water. It was silly trying to talk himself out of an admission he had made already. They had admitted to each other that they feared for Mum's safety. Once spoken, nothing could take it back.

'How about bed, sis?' he stammered, in a whirl for words that might patch the damage. 'You'll be better in bed. It's only because we're out here that we're thinking up all sorts of rubbish. We ought to be in bed snoring our heads off. Nothing can happen to Mum. Mum's never dented a fender; Dad's never scratched the paint. We're carrying on like a couple of ninnies.'

She shook in his arms and suddenly, in his mind, Max stood off a distance and watched himself comforting her. To become aware of himself was to sense the responsibility. What he saw pleased him because Brenda as a rule was so domineering. It was not unpleasant to discover that Brenda could be soft enough to show it. Even while he watched himself he seemed to grow a couple of inches.

'Yeh,' he said firmly, 'bed, sis. Enough of this rot.'

He drew her after him a few shuffling steps.

'No,' she said.

'Come on.' He propelled her to her room. 'You hop into bed. I'll clean up the mess.'

To his astonishment she did as he said, and having committed himself he then bustled with forced conviction from job to job so that she could hear his movements. He washed the cups, put things away, swept up the crumbs, turned off the radiator, blew out the candle, and more like a man than a boy trembling with doubt made his own way back to bed.

The sheets were as cold as a plunge in the lake and Tony was snoring his head off. Max pulled the blankets over his ears to shut out the silence and all the sounds that might move across it. If anything *was* going on he wanted to hear nothing of it. In private a fellow didn't need to be a hero; in private he could be himself.

FOUR

'Speed it Thru Mac'

ALISON'S FATHER seemed to fragment in the mist; he appeared to fall apart in pieces and vanish from sight.

It was so extraordinary the way it happened that she almost called out, 'Dad, don't . . .' but didn't, because for a moment or two beyond it she saw the torch-glow moving across her sight, across the invisible curve of the hairpin bend, going down like a distant light at sea sliding into a trough.

Then there was silence, but not absolute. There were creakings in the vehicle, perhaps minute movements against the brakes; creakings in the engine, perhaps of cold air over hot metals; creakings outside of living trees labouring in the frost.

'Dad, don't. . . . Don't go away.' But by then he was gone.

He had left the door open and for a while she wished he had shut it, but she was reluctant to touch it herself. There was a crackling barrier between her and her father that she had never felt before, never sensed, and only a hair-thin bridge across. She couldn't bring herself to reach over and slam the door shut because while it remained open she was not completely cut off. But she didn't know what she wanted at heart; the warmth of the cabin or the warmth of the bond with her father reaching out tenuously into the fog; a bond now so thin it was like a thread of silk threatening to break. Something was happening to her, something strange and unwelcome that was colder than the night.

Never, never in her life had she been lost, but she was lost now. This was what it was like to be alone in a place where everything was strange and no one knew the way home. Somehow she had stepped out of line, turned a corner that she couldn't remember, crossed a road she hadn't seen. Dad should have stopped her. Surely he had known? Didn't he care? Or was he fed up with her, tagging along, spoiling his style? She was not a little girl now, blind to his faults, ignoring his weaknesses. There was nothing special about him at all except his vanity; mutton dressing up as lamb, grey hairs plucked out so they wouldn't show, flirting with her school-mates like a kid of nineteen.

'Oh, Dad. . . . Is it you, or is it me?'

She wished he would come back, she pleaded for the glow of the torch to reappear in the fog, sure that the need for him to hurry was urgent or he would be too late. For what, she didn't know.

'I'm freezing,' she hissed, with a violent change of humour. 'He should have shut the door; it was *selfish* of him to leave it like that. Why should I sit here freezing to death?'

But he didn't come.

'What's he doing? It's minutes since he left.'

She released her safety belt and pushed across the seat to the open door intending irritably to pull it shut, but something held her back. Out there it was bitter; even here the fog was raw in her throat.

'Dad,' she called. 'Are you coming?'

Fog seemed to wrap her voice into a box to prevent it from getting out.

'Dad!'

He could have stepped to the edge of a cliff and dropped off. He could have stumbled and broken a leg. He could have been waylaid and knocked out.

'What's he doing to me? He shouldn't walk away and not come back. Walking off into fog and not coming back. Dad! Answer me!'

It was crazy spending every holiday imprisoned in a truck or sitting stupidly, half-awake, in cafés blue with smoke in the middle of the night listening to the horse-talk or family-talk of grown-up men (laughing about their kids, complaining about their wives), or staring with eyes that stung at black roads and other people's window-panes and blinding headlamps that soared over crests like explosions of light. A head that ached and a stomach that hurt and boredom like a year in a cell. Surrounded by adult noise, by rattles and crashes and bangs and shouts.

'Dad!'

She grabbed the door at the limit of her reach to slam it shut, but it stayed wide open, stuck, too heavy to shift.

'Why *doesn't* he come back?'

Suddenly, he was there, a pale-red glow like something from an unknown world coming up out of the earth. The glow became the face of the torch distorted by smears and dribbles on the windscreen and she slid back across the seat, hurriedly, half-ashamed of her thoughts, not looking at first. She heard him scraping his feet to shift the mud from his boots, felt the weight of his body strike the step, and his presence fill the cab. The door slammed like a rifle shot, making her jump.

He was panting for breath, clearing phlegm from his throat, sniffing, rubbing with his hands his eyes and his nose. She shuddered, though she tried hard not to.

'Should have shut the door, love,' he said, 'weren't you cold? Letting the fog get in. It's a *shocking* night out. Got a hanky?'

'Tissues,' she said, and passed him the box.

He blew his nose several times then sat back while his breathing evened out. 'Gets into you, that stuff, like bits of glass.'

'Didn't you hear me calling?'

'No, love.'

'You took an awfully long time.'

'Did I? Sorry, love.'

'Where did you go?' she said, in a way accusing him.

'Down the hill a bit to have a look. We'll get round all

right, with a bit of luck. Got to, haven't we? whether we like it or not. Dangerous; stuck here like this. Safety belt on, love. Buckle it up.'

The starter motor struck like an anvil and the engine returned to life. 'Something wearing there,' he said, 'I'll have to look at that.'

She didn't know what he was talking about, but buckled her belt.

The transport began to creep a little against the brakes. 'Do you want to get out?' he said.

'Why?'

'You might think yourself safer out than in.'

'That's silly, Dad. I always feel safe with you.'

Perhaps he sounded hoarse. 'That's what I thought myself until tonight.'

She almost let it pass, but said, 'That's an odd thing to say about me.'

'Is it?' He sighed. 'My imagination I guess. I could have driven all night until this happened. Hold-ups wear me thin.' She sensed a weary sort of smile in the dark. 'Or is it now you're more of a woman than a girl?'

He let the brake go, suddenly, it seemed to her, and in bottom gear with lights dipped swung close to the ditch at the foot of the cutting on the high side of the turn.

'Wind your window down, love, if you don't mind. Listen out for the scrape. I'll need to hit the bank for every inch I can scrounge. I want to do it in one turn if I can without backing up for a second bite.'

He drifted closer, the cab scratching through twigs and leaves, until they felt something grab like a hand, the sharp edge of the trailer spading into the ground. He braked and Alison was shaking inside, not only because of the night and the fog and the turn, but because of Dad.

'Torch, love,' he said, 'poke your head out and have a look. No rocks? No tree trunks in the way?'

She checked as best as she could; it was difficult to see through the leaves; it was hard to avoid spiking her eyes; but the corner of the tray had scored a mark about a foot long and two or three inches deep in the bank at the side, dislodging pebbles and moss and lumps of dirt into the ditch below. 'It's all right,' she said thinly, 'I think; if you keep your wheels out of the ditch. There's not much to spare.'

'Ridiculous. A ditch on a turn like this.'

'It's there, Dad.'

'I know it's there and the idiot responsible for it ought to be kicked.' He paused. 'Give the windscreen a wipe, love. I can't see out properly.'

She wiped it for him with the big soft cloth, but leaning across him caught a sharpness in his breath that set her back nervously in her seat. He was scared. He *wasn't* sure, 'bit of luck' or not.

He crept, winding hard like a helmsman on a ship, sitting bolt upright, hissing through his teeth, scraping painfully through leaves (a tearing sound), jolting the brakes, straining his neck to see out; his lights flooding scrub and tree trunks that seemed to be falling continually into a pit.

Two-thirds of the way round he stopped, with a sideways slip of at least a foot, unmistakably felt, before the vehicle came to rest. 'That's that!' His voice was high-pitched. 'Missed by yards. I've *got* to back up for a second try.'

'Dad . . .' But she did not pursue the thought; let it fade weakly into the throbbing engine sound. Her feet were thrust into the floor against imaginary brakes. He reversed and crept back but the wheels spun.

'Mud,' he grunted. Perhaps for her benefit perhaps for himself.

He tried again, but again slipped the wheels, slewing sideways probably another foot. He stopped with a curse she could hear.

After a while he hissed, 'Wouldn't it *rip* you!' Then for a minute at least said nothing, but sat straight, perhaps sweating, perhaps shivering, and she wished almost frantically to know what was going on.

'If you do get round, Dad,' she said timidly, 'how will you turn the corner again coming back up?'

'Sit tight. Your dad's no mug. I'm getting my wind.'

'There might be more turns like this farther down.'

'Don't you wish that on me, love!'

He gunned the accelerator (to her wild surprise) pelting showers of mud and stones like hail against metal, jolting, skidding sickeningly underneath, then cracked the gear lever across and lurched forward with the steering wheel spinning through his hands of its own accord.

It was reckless; she knew in her heart it was inexplicable; then felt a jolt that came like a blow in her back; a screech of metal protesting against something supposed not to happen, a tearing of wood, of leaves, of rending sticks, but the cab seemed to be going ahead as it should have done round the turn, close to the edge, on the brink, judged to the inch, with foliage whipping the side window, shedding bits.

He was round; he had made it downhill on to the straight; she couldn't understand it because fright like beating wings inside her told her it couldn't be true, that something was wrong, that something wasn't right; running straight but jolting with tearing sounds in the scrub, as though another vehicle driven wildly ran beside them or had rammed them in the rear. She heard his shout and felt the crack somewhere behind her that almost broke her neck, only half-felt the gigantic wrench that spun the transport, rearing grotesquely, over the edge, then felt only sounds inside her head, sounds like rolling thunders and breaking waves and distant gunfire becoming more distant. Then felt nothing.

FIVE

The Older of the Two

MAX SENSED THE weight falling and a hand fell near his shoulder like ten pounds of lead.

It shouldn't have startled him, but it did, it scared him half out of his wits and he leapt up swinging an arm that connected with flesh and bone, hurting her and hurting himself. Brenda yelped.

He had known it would be her, that she would come, but every nerve of his body was on edge, every motion he went through was a big act, every word stammered was a defence against panic, because his brain was not functioning as it should have done, his brain was stifled by something racing in his blood. Yet there was nothing that Brenda could tell him that he could not have told her himself. There was a sound on the hill that wrenched his heart, a multiplicity of sounds, of crashes, of thuds a long way off or muted by fog. Bewildering sounds that didn't add up.

'Do you hear it?' she said, almost spitting it out, with judgement in her voice, with breathlessness from her rush through the house. 'Now tell me there's nothing wrong.'

'Hear what?' Fighting for time to master himself.

'Listen. Listen.'

'To what?' he wailed.

How could he deny it while it thudded on the hill (Lord, how it thudded; what in heaven was it) as though boulders as big as house-tops were bouncing up and down?

'*What is it, Max!*' Brenda screeched then answered herself hysterically. 'It's an accident, isn't it? It's Mum and Dad because it can't be anyone else. They've gone over the edge. They've driven over in the fog, rolling over and over down the hill.'

'*Stop it!*' he shouted.

She fell silent to a point, panting in the dark, shivering so violently that he was frightened for her.

'There's nothing,' he said stupidly, dully, because by then there wasn't. 'I can't hear a thing. Can you?'

'You liar, Max; you yellow belly.' She, too, was fighting to master herself. 'You were hiding under the blanket, weren't you!' Not a question that time, but a statement. 'There was an awful crash, crash after crash. For a while the engine again and then crash.'

There was a mumble in the small, congested space as of someone waking up.

'It's Tony,' Max whispered fiercely, 'now Tortoise is awake. It'll be David next.'

Brenda went, he heard her go, though he couldn't see a thing, and groped after her into the living room. Everything had sharp corners; dressing-table, door jambs, and the seats of chairs. He blundered into them, adding pain to fright.

'Light the candle,' she said, in a tone of voice that a judge might use to pronounce a sentence of death.

She was boss again. Her moods changed so quickly that she muddled him, on top of his hurts, on top of his panic. For the second time that night he was close to tears, but of a different sort.

'I don't know where I am,' he stammered, 'I can't see in the dark.'

'Light the *candle*.'

'Blow you, Brenda.' There was desperation in him that broke in his voice with a squeak. 'I can't find the bloomin' thing.'

Tony called thickly, 'What's goin' on?'

'Be quiet,' Max shrilled, welcoming the venting of his anger in a direction that wouldn't snap back. 'You'll wake David, you twit.'

'What's goin' on out there?' Tony called. 'Whatcha doing out of bed?' A thin beam of light like a question played across the doorway of the room they had left. 'What's all the noise?'

'You're all the noise,' bawled Brenda, 'for heaven's sake be quiet, like Max says.'

'Where's Mum? Where's Dad? What's everybody doing up?'

'He's hopeless,' Brenda cried, 'once he starts you can never shut him up. He's so *stupid*. Light that candle, Max, for heaven's sake. This is awful.'

Tony came blundering out, crashing his shoulder against the door, waving the beam of his midget torch in everyone's eyes. 'Whatcha all doing out here? Don't you believe in light? Why don't you switch it on?'

Max at last struck a match that didn't break and put it to the candle. 'The batteries are flat, you blockhead. What d'you think? Now shut up before you wake David.'

'Whatcha all doing out here? What time is it? Whatcha wake a fella up for at this hour?'

'Please, Tortoise,' pleaded Brenda, 'there's been an accident.'

He stood there grimacing, scratching his stomach, with his hair standing up like straw. Tony was no oil painting even in the full light of day. He hadn't really heard a word; if he had, Max's harshness would have hurt like a wound. A banging on the wall came from David's room.

'That's *done* it,' moaned Max. 'David's awake. Now what'll we do?'

'Blow David,' cried Brenda, 'you're worrying all the time about David. He's safe in bed. What about Mum and Dad?'

'What about Mum and Dad?' said Tony.

'There's been an accident. Didn't you hear me say? Accident, accident, accident; and no one seems to care. Are you all stupid?'

'Accident,' said Tony, 'what accident? I wish someone would stop David bangin' on the wall. *Turn it up, David.* You'll wake Mum and Dad.'

Brenda's brittle mood broke to a sob, 'Doesn't anyone

understand? What's wrong with you all? Max, you're the eldest, you're the *man*.'

But Max couldn't think while David continued to bang on the wall, at first with his fists and then with his feet. David never seemed to feel the cold, no matter what the hour. He always woke the house that way, every morning, at about six. David often laughed for joy as he banged on the wall and he started laughing now.

Brenda pressed the palms of her hands flat to her ears and hurried, distracted, to the outside door. She unlatched it clumsily and stepped on to the ramp in the open air. Of the cold, bitter enough to hit her with a physical blow, she was unaware. She padded in bare feet, her hand instinctively to the rail down to the ground.

'Mum!' she called, in a frantic sort of way. 'Dad!'

But nothing was to be heard except that persistent thudding on David's bedroom wall. It pursued her blindly like a command for fifty or sixty yards. Then she found herself, by surprise, on what must have been the road, confined, wrapped about with fog and stillness and intense cold. All movement in the house was muffled and for the moment she was not sure in which direction it lay. There was a sudden impulse to grope with her hands, to swim out of that faintly luminous mist backlit by a stark full moon somewhere or other up top in a silvered sky. But she knew there was no getting out of it until day, until sunshine began to work through. She could have leapt into it as into a bottomless pool. She could have been sinking into it down and down.

'Mum! Mum!'

There was no answering call.

'Oh, Mum. Don't die.'

She seemed to be frozen in a sheath of ice; suddenly she knew her feet were bare, that her gown was tossed over a chair in her room, that she wore only her nightdress damply reaching the ground, that standing here was mad, that David, back there, was still hammering on his wall.

'Oh, Mum, what will we do with David if something has happened to you?'

'Are you there, Brenda?' It was Max, his voice distorted as though speaking into a tube.

'Yes,' she said.

'Come back. You'll catch your death. Come and get some clothes on, then we'll go.'

'Go where?'

'To look for them, of course. Isn't that what you want to do?'

She didn't know; she really didn't know. Crying out for Mum was one thing; searching in the fog another. There was always a faint hope while the fact of an accident was not sure. Once they knew, once they found the wreckage crushed against a tree or deep in a gully upside down. . . .

'Come on, Brenda. Don't be a fool. You can't go it alone.'

'I'm coming.'

'Where are you?'

'On the road. I'm coming.'

'You're not coming, you clown. You're walking farther away.'

She stopped, confused, because there was no doubt that Max's urgent voice was harder to hear.

'Where are you, Max?'

'Here. Are you still on the road?'

'I can't see. I don't know.'

'For cryin' out loud,' he yelled. 'Come back *this* way, towards the house.'

'I don't know where the house is.'

There was a silence, then another call. 'Can you see any trees?'

Her voice caught a bit, perhaps from the fog she could feel in her lungs. 'I can't see anything. It's cold, Max.'

'Is the ground sloping down.'

'Up and down. It depends which way you go.'

'You must be below the road. Turn round and come uphill, back here.'

'Wave the torch, Max.'

'I haven't got the torch. It's with Tony in the house.'

'Well, get it, please. I don't like it here.'

'Golly, Brenda,' he yelled, 'what a thing to do.'

She waited for him, shaking from cold, afraid of the lake which must be near, lifting her feet in turn to get them off the ground. It was awful. '*Mum!*' she shrieked, frantically, desperately, but nothing came back, only Max's call: 'Can you see me now?'

She looked everywhere into depthless haze. 'No . . .'

He swore with passion, then yelled, 'I'm coming down to the road.' But it wasn't an angry yell; the swear word hadn't really been directed at her.

'Can you see me now?'

'No.'

'Now?'

'*No!*'

'Golly, Brenda, this is mad.' She heard him cough. 'Blow you, Brenda. Fancy getting lost now. How far away are you?'

Suddenly she saw a glow. 'I see you,' she screamed. 'Oh, Max.' She stumbled towards the light, crying. Until then she had been dry-eyed. She snatched his arm and clung to him and he almost dragged her back towards the house. 'Strike me,' he said, 'what a thing to do. Are you mad?'

He bundled her up the ramp, hardening to her sobs (he was shaking from fright) and pushed her inside. 'Get some clothes on. Bloomin' girls!'

Tony was holding David's hand. He couldn't let go now that he had brought David from his room. For much of the time, when David was up and about, someone had to hold him by the hand or he pulled things down and threw them, or tore things up, or ran for the door. He was pulling on Tony's hand in an arc from side to side, swinging for the fun of it; a beautiful small boy nine years old, who looked five. He said something that sounded like Brenda's name but she brushed past him. 'Put him back in his room,' Brenda said, 'what the dickens did you bring him out for?'

Tony looked hurt. 'It's the only way I could stop him kicking. I thought I was doing the right thing. A fella can never please you.'

'Put him in his room,' Brenda called, and slammed her own door.

'Don't take any notice of her,' Max said. 'You're doin' all right, Tortoise. Hang on to him; I've got to change too.'

'What about me?'

'Crikey, you can't come. You'll have to stay here.'

'*On my own?*'

'Yeh. Someone's got to stay with David. We're not goin' to a party, you know.' Max suddenly felt like crying again. 'Gee, Tortoise. . . . If it's Mum and Dad, what'll we do?' He couldn't trust himself another moment and rushed into his room.

The wall, to Tony, was like a railway carriage, people rushing into it and slamming doors. Everybody was going away and leaving him at home. Behind their doors they were floundering round in the dark looking for clothes. Brenda was crying. Max was making sounds of a kind he had not made since he was a little boy. Tony couldn't remember when he had heard Max cry before. It wasn't like a girl's cry, or his own, it was a grating sound, deep down, sadder than all the sorrows in the world. Max was fifteen years and seven months old, as tall as a man. Max could run like a hare and bowl a faster ball than any other kid in his form. Max was a god; he had brains to spare. He helped Tony with his homework. He could play a guitar. To stand in his shadow, to declare: 'That's Max, my big brother,' was like having a famous athlete in the family tree. But Max was crying. Tony threw his arms round David and hugged him. 'Golly, Fatso,' he said, 'I reckon it's on the square; something's happened to Mum and Dad.' But David did not appear to understand.

Brenda's door opened and she came out sniffling, bleary-eyed, with a beret pulled down over her disordered hair, a heavy jumper on back to front, her nightdress still showing, stuffed into her jeans, and walking shoes under one arm. She said nothing to Tony.

'Sis,' he said.

But she ignored him and started lacing up her shoes with one foot to a chair.

'Sis,' he said, 'are we orphans?'

She snapped, 'Of course not.'

'If Mum and Dad are dead we've got to be, haven't we?'

'They're *not* dead.'

'You said they were.'

'I didn't, I didn't. I didn't say any such thing. I said there'd been an accident; we heard it, I don't even know where; that doesn't mean they're dead.'

David started laughing as he often did and struggled to break free from Tony's hug.

'Put him in his room,' Brenda cried. 'Why don't you do as you're told? Put him in there and snib the door.'

'I can't,' Tony whimpered, 'he's too strong for me.'

'Too strong for you, my eye. You're built like a bullock. Give him to me.' She grabbed David by an arm and almost threw him into his room. 'Now leave him there. You don't have to nurse him like a sick pet; let him kick the wall. We can't be worried by David at a time like this.'

'You're cruel,' Tony flared, '*cruel* and mean. You're not my boss. You're not Mum yet. I'll do as I please.'

'You'll do as I say or feel my hand.' Then she sobbed, and saw Max standing there looking fierce. 'I'm sorry,' she cried, 'I'm all muddled up . . .'

'You sure are.' He shook his head like an old man. 'I reckon the place for you is here. I don't want you with me. Get your clothes on, Tony.'

Brenda tossed her head to hide her shame. 'Don't you speak to me like that.'

'Listen, sis. From now on I reckon I'll be speaking to you as I bally well choose. Get those clothes on, Tony. Hurry up, Tortoise. Shake a leg.'

(Tony would have walked through fire if Max had been at his side.)

'I've got to come,' Brenda cried, 'I've *got* to. You can't leave me here.'

Max hardened to her more. 'Fat lot of use you'd be up there. You can't step out of the door without losing your way.'

'Max, that's not fair.'

'What's *fair* got to do with it? *Fair's* the word you should be thinking of when you knock David around.'

'I never knock David around.'

'What were you doing a minute ago?'

'Please, Max, don't hold that against me. He was laughing. Don't be cruel.'

Tony floundered out, hopping, jamming a foot into a shoe, with clothes on all ways, dragging his overcoat by one sleeve.

'You can't take Tony. He's only eleven years old. You can't take a little kid up there. You don't know what you'll find.'

'Little kid?' Tony squealed. '*Me?*'

'You can't, Max, you can't.' Brenda was still in tears.

'I've got to, haven't I?' he said. 'I'd be crackers to take you. Have you got any spare batteries, Tony? That torch will have some work to do.'

'Sure; I've got spares.'

'Bring 'em, and grab my watch off the shelf. I think it's there.'

'It's twenty-five past two,' Brenda announced, 'if you want to know the time.' Then headed with determination for the outside door. Max blocked her way. She stood up against him, trembling, red-eyed, an impulse short of blows. 'It's got to be Mum and Dad,' she said viciously, 'can't you see? He's never missed the train. They'd have been back by now. It's two *hours*.'

Max knew. He didn't have to be told.

'They could be dying up there,' she said, 'while we're arguing here.' Then she seemed to shrink from him, to become small. 'I'm sorry about everything, Max, you know I am. The things you've said are awfully unkind. They're so untrue. If you leave me here I think I'll scream. I couldn't bear to be left alone. Don't take Tony, please.'

Tony was waiting, with torch batteries in hand, with Max's watch, with an appeal in his eyes that made it even harder to say, 'Sorry, Tortoise, but Brenda *is* older than you.' Max had to look away. 'Make sure David's o.k., in bed, tucked up warm.'

Suddenly, Tony was alone.

They had taken his batteries, emptied his hands; their

heavy footsteps, slipping a little, were thudding on the ramp, thudding away, then gone.

His head was in a whirl, his cheeks were flushed. He was all dressed up with nowhere to go. There'd been so much anger, so many tears, so many changes of mind.

What about Mum and Dad?

He gaped into the silence, stunned to be alone. Everything was lifeless except for the leaning candle flame, elongated, like a falling star tethered to an inch of wax, tugging to break free. They'd said the electric light was finished, the batteries flat. Was there another candle in the house? If not, one inch more of wax to burn and then the night would be black.

What about Mum and Dad?

They should have all gone, all of them together, Tony, Brenda and Max, to look for Mum and Dad.

'Hey, Mum. Hey, Dad.'

Fog drifted in like a genie through the open door and David's presence—a different sort of cloud—crept through to Tony from behind the living-room wall. David crying, an unusual sound.

'Hey, David,' Tony said, 'what you crying for? Your big brother's here.'

SIX

A Dome Battened Down

THE FOG SEEMED to be full of obstacles that didn't quite hit them, tree trunks, branches, blank brick walls—an utter impossibility. It was the centre of the road, pot-holed now (once a carefully graded crown) and they *knew* nothing was there. How could anything be there? The middle of the road, open air. They stumbled a bit, flinching, feeling an urge to walk sideways, to squeeze through fence posts, wires, and hedges with prickles on, that weren't there.

'Stick beside me,' Max said, 'better give me your hand.'

It was a cold hand, almost shy, but it was alive. ('If we'd all gone in the car that hand would be dead. Hers. Mine. Both hands would be dead. Oh, Brenda, I'd hate you to be dead.')

'I'm sorry, Max, about everything.'

He almost missed the fork away from the waterfront, to the left, turning uphill. He turned by instinct a few yards late and had to scramble with her across the frozen bank, blades of grass as stiff as splinters crackling beneath their feet.

'You don't have to be sorry, sis,' he said. 'It's forgotten. I was no better myself.'

Tony's cheap little torch spilled a timid pool of light at their feet.

'It's not much use, is it?' Max said.

'No.'

When he raised the beam it scarcely reached the side of the road; the light bled out against a mass of darkness and barely trickled under it into mist and silence. A whole world could have been out there and they would not have known.

'We won't see them, will we?' Brenda said, 'if they're off the road.'

'And that's where they are. We know they are. But not down here, sis. We've a long way to go yet.'

'I can't believe it,' she whispered, 'not Mum and Dad.'

Max choked. 'It happens to other people all the time.'

Each clung to the other's hand.

'Your heavy shoes?' he asked hoarsely.

'Yeh.'

'I wonder whether we should head off uphill, through the bush?'

Her 'No', was almost explosive. 'Keep to the road, Max. I got lost before, without trying.'

He turned to her vaguely. 'Yeh, we've got to take care.'

They walked heavily, almost dragging each other, but warmth was creeping into their hands, palm to palm, though wrapped about with cold.

'We'd better run, sis. Just a jog, eh? Come on.'

But with deeper breaths the fog was rawer still, too raw for human lungs. They jogged a couple of hundred yards through the first upward curve, then slowed to a walk of nervy haste, as fast as legs that wanted to give at the knees could be pushed.

'Crikey, sis,' he panted, 'I wonder how far? Maybe a couple of miles. Maybe as far as the hairpin bend. I wonder if it's really there?'

After a pause, a long pause of shuffling uphill: 'We don't know, do we?' she said. 'Not with the fog. There's no saying what fog does with sound.'

'I can't work out the thuds, sis. The car couldn't have rolled like that, down and down.'

'It's steep below the bend; almost too steep to stand.'

'Yeh,' he said.

'Or it might have been a rockfall. You never know.

They might have started it. They might have rammed something. They might still be on the road.'

'Dad travels too fast,' Max said. (He had never believed it before.) 'He drives it like a blooming racing car. It had to happen, sis. It had to happen someday. I think he reckons if he got through the war there's nothing that can touch him now.'

'Mum's just as bad.'

'Gran's always at him to slow down.'

The fog was hurting. Inside it began to feel like a saw and outside it was an irritant in their eyes.

'We'd better stick to the edge of the road, she said. 'Keep the light down. Look for signs.'

'We're not far enough up. There'd be nothing yet.'

'If they went straight over there mightn't even be a skid.'

Max stopped, his mind in turmoil. Desperately, he wanted to cry; but the part of him that was almost a man categorically refused to allow it to happen a second time. Brenda waited, hanging on his hand, no longer capable of deeper thought at all; inside her was a storm only of noise.

'Dad!' Max screamed. '*Dad, Dad, Dad.*'

There was no echo, no sense of space lying out there through which the scream could explore. Mist was a smother, an enveloping blanket, an ice dome battened down.

'Crikey, sis, if he's alive he must have heard.'

She said nothing (his scream was sounding on inside her), but she tugged a little on his hand to go on. Somehow, he had never loved her quite so much before. It would have been terrible with Tony. Tony would have talked hesitantly all the time, questioning this and questioning that, like a slow bird trying out new sounds. He would have held Max by the hand, too, but it would have been there to drain strength away, not to feed it through.

'Gee, Fatso,' Tony said, 'Don't perform.'

He tried the door but it opened only an inch or two because David had his back to the other side.

'Hey; get away from the door.'

But David was like a sack of grain, a soft, unmoving weight unwilling to yield. David could be stubborn at times; like a donkey that wanted to sit down.

'Come on, Fatso. I'm not goin' to hurt you. I'm not goin' to growl. I'm not a grump like sis.'

He relaxed from the door to encourage David to do the same, but immediately it whacked shut and stayed firm.

'Don't be mean, David.'

But David wouldn't move.

'I'll push,' Tony threatened. 'I'll push like mad and then you'll know.'

But David sobbed to himself, his back to the door, and didn't really hear a word, and Tony slid down, right there, his own back to the opposite side; back to back with wood between them, farther apart than a hundred miles.

He wanted to cuddle David to make him feel better, so he wouldn't cry any more. And he wanted David for himself, to have him there soft and warm, to help him to be brave. He didn't want to be alone. It was cold all alone, and empty, like being in a huge hall before the crowd arrived, and creepy with fog still coming in through the outside door. It was a long, long journey across the room to the outside door; so far he didn't want to go alone. Going with Fatso wouldn't be so bad. He didn't mind going with Fatso anywhere at all, any time, so long as other kids that he knew weren't around. Then it was different, somehow. Fatso held his hand and *never* tried to run away. From Brenda and Max he often struggled to break free. With Tony he only laughed to himself, or smiled, or talked in a language of his own, and plodded patiently, awkwardly, faithfully beside him.

'Gee, Fatso, be a pal. Shove away from the door.'

But nothing changed. David didn't move. He was never a lump of jelly that could be pushed at will from here to there; he was harder to push than the little kids at school. *They* did as they were told because if they didn't they got a thump on the ear. David had a will of his own, though grown-up people who didn't know him well thought he was a *vegetable*; it was a word some of them had used. David wasn't a carrot or a cauliflower; Tony knew—better than others knew—that something inside David thought with words, but the words never came out in a way that anyone could understand.

'You'll get cold, sitting here,' Tony said. 'Look, Fatso, you've *got* to move.' It wasn't an order, not really; it was a plea.

What would they do if Mum and Dad didn't come home? Just never came? Just stopped being around as if they had never been?

Like Sid Gore's Mum and Dad who went rock-fishing at Rye and were swept out to sea in a freak wave. Sid had great big eyes like plates, like black holes in his head. Sid went with his sisters to live with their Gran a long way away and never came back to school again. The Gore kids sort of melted into thin air when they didn't have a Mum and Dad. Hardly anyone remembered them any more. Tony couldn't remember anything about Sid except his great big eyes, big black holes.

An arm seemed to reach out of Tony's heart, hurting as it reached farther and farther out. On the end of it was a hand wildly snatching for things to hang on to, but no matter where it snatched nothing was there.

'Fatso; please open the door.'

But David wouldn't move.

Then something drew Tony's eyes to the candle. Instant by instant the flame grew larger and larger, instant by instant widening his surprise. Suddenly it disappeared.

A thud of fright almost took his breath away.

'No,' he called, as though by command he could recall the flame that had gone. But the flame didn't stir, didn't rise up again.

An overwhelming sense of isolation seized Tony, as though he had missed by inches the last bus home; as though he had run for it madly, miles across country through the rain.

Again and again they called. 'Mum! Dad!'

Sometimes they called stridently, demanding an answer, as though nothing, not even the dead, would dare to be silent. Sometimes they called hoarsely, crying for a response that nothing alive could have refused. But only trees heard, only frosted leaves, only shivering birds, only harmless little animals they couldn't see.

'Where are we?'

Max sighed. 'Search me.'

The torchlight showed them only the gravel at their feet. 'Do put the other batteries in,' Brenda urged wearily, time and again.

'We've got to save them. Crikey, sis, we can't be left up here without light. There's no knowing how much we'll need it later on.'

'We need it *now*. We can't *look* if we can't see.'

It was an awful decision to have to face. 'It's such a little torch, Brenda; it's only good for such a short time.'

'We need it *now*.'

'Wait till we get to the hairpin bend. It can't be more than half a mile.'

They were not warm; they couldn't move fast enough to keep warm although they pushed themselves as hard as they could. Nor could they speak with comfort; they were hoarse from fog. The only hot spot where life sparked was at the joining of their palms. Cold, like teeth, bit at their noses, ears, chins, feet, and the backs of their hands.

'It's nearly three o'clock,' Max said, 'there's no doubt now, is there?'

'Unless Dad missed the train.'

Max tried to add up minutes against the beating in his head. It was almost like a physical pain. 'Crikey, sis, it doesn't leave until eight and he's away from work by five. It's at Hamer by twenty past one. He's never missed the train.'

The minutes ticked over in his head, lining up in rows. 'And would it matter if he had? Would Mum have camped there for the night? She could have driven home backwards in the time that's gone. She wouldn't take a hundred minutes for thirty miles. She's got fog lights. She knows the road. Anyway, he wouldn't have missed the train. He didn't miss it, sis. You know that. So do I.'

There was no light from the torch any more.

'Do you reckon we can see without it?' he said.

'No, Max, no, no, no.'

She sounded worn out, frail; much, much older than fourteen years and he was having to lead her while her feet dragged. The moon was up there as it had been before, somewhere, but it lit without detail an opalescent cloud and the cloud was the world.

He stopped and Brenda slid from his hand, slid on to the road where she sat like a little girl lost, quietly crying, awfully afraid of what must be close by. Earnestly, she wanted Max to take no notice of her, but he dropped beside her. 'Do you want to stay here?' he said. 'Shall I go on alone?' And having said it he realized how foolish it was. His arm went around her and they sat in a huddle, swaying a little from side to side.

'I won't go without you,' he said, but heard his voice as though someone else had spoken. All the flesh and blood things of himself seemed to be miles away, almost out of feeling, out of hearing, and out of sight. He didn't really know what he was doing, any more than Brenda knew. None of it was happening; it was vague like a dream; it was as liquid as a dream flowing for a few moments one way and then another. Then something hit his brain with a crack, sickening him. *He was falling asleep.*

He jolted his eyes open, panting, 'Brenda,' he called, 'Wake up! I've lost the torch. I've dropped the torch. I can't find it.' His hands were groping on the road, frantically, but even as he groped his right hand still held the torch, clenched about it, locked about it, almost frozen to it. The discovery made him angry.

'I'm cold,' Brenda said.

He jerked her to her feet and said viciously, 'Come on, come on, come on; we'll die if we stay here.' But he couldn't see; the world was an opalescent cloud; and he had to stop to fumble with the torch to put the new batteries in it. He didn't know that Brenda wasn't with him until he heard her shriek. Then he realized she had walked on.

'Max!'

'Yes!' Breathless and sharp. 'Where are you?'

'There's something here.'

'Something where? What?'

'It's metal. I tripped over it. There's a great lump of metal in the road.'

Max didn't want to move. He was almost afraid to breathe. 'Is it part of the car?' Every word was agony to say. There was a terror in him that urged him to turn and run off downhill. He had asked but he didn't want to know.

She answered almost then, but it seemed like an hour. 'I think it's a drum, the sort you put oil in. A big metal drum. What's it doing here? It's had a terrible thump.'

He stumbled to where he thought she was.

'Max,' she cried, 'there's something in it. It rattles. There's a funny smell.'

He couldn't find her. He couldn't see her. 'Where are you?'

'Here, here!'

'I don't know where "here" is.'

'Against the bank. Use your torch. Hurry, Max, hurry. It's an awfully funny smell.'

'I haven't *fixed* the torch. The bloomin' thing's in bits.'

'Well, fix it!' Suddenly she sounded as she had an hour ago. She was Brenda again, that bossy, bumptious bit of goods. 'I told and told you to put the batteries in. *Hurry*, Max.'

He fumbled and panted and his hands were so cold he could scarcely do anything with them. They felt as big as hams, as useless as blocks of wood, and when Brenda got that tone in her voice she always muddled him up.

'Maybe it's not Mum at all,' she said. '*Maybe it was a truck.*'

Something strange was happening, an extraordinary change of mood that was breaking Max's self-control. He had carried a terrible load; he knew he had carried it well. The change of mood was in Brenda and something about it was cruel, belittling him. It would have been better if he could have seen her, then he would have known for sure, would have been able to shake her out of it before it set in.

It was awful coping with Brenda in the middle of a fog. She wasn't like a boy; boys weren't complicated.

He sensed a peculiar smile that he didn't like; it was in her voice and mood and radiated from her like transmissions of energy. The torchlight poured from Max's hand and Brenda sounded shrill. 'I told you it was a truck. Didn't I?'

He found her against the bank, actually in the ditch, with her hands on her hips like a big, brassy blonde, her head slanted almost with vulgarity at the light; not the gentle Brenda he had drawn along beside him, palm to palm.

'See,' she said, 'it's a drum. It's fallen from a truck. There hasn't been an accident at all. It's the drum we heard crashing downhill. Any boy worth his salt would have known.'

'That's not fair,' he stammered.

'Not fair, my eye. All this panic.'

'There must have been an accident,' he wailed. 'We *heard* it, Brenda. We couldn't imagine *that*. And if there's a truck it'd have to be here. Where is it? You're barmy carrying on like this. Mum and Dad are still an hour late. Maybe Dad brought the drum from town. Nothing's changed.'

'Everything's changed,' Brenda snapped. 'It's a truck, you drip, lost its load on the bend. The truck'll be higher uphill.'

She took the torch from him and directed it on to the drum. 'See,' she said. 'Would Dad have brought *that*?'

Inside her, everything was cheering. She didn't want to be hard on Max, she wanted to shout for joy as fiercely as she could, but it all came out wrong, as it often did.

'How could it be a truck?' Max wailed, his voice thin. 'What would a truck be doing here at three o'clock in the morning or at three o'clock any time? For Pete's sake, sis, grow up.'

'A ten-gallon drum,' she said, 'the sort they put oil in.' Then her voice caught. She seemed to choke and all the cheering inside stopped dead. It was a drum painted white with stark letters in black. She had to bend to read them, and, stunned, read them twice, pushing the drum with her foot. POISON. POTASSIUM CYANIDE.

The drum was partly crushed. It had struck a rock. There was a spill in the ditch where she stood, powder and flakes and dirty white marbles.

Suddenly, she tossed the torch from her and stumbled backwards, thrusting out her arms, extending her fingers as though she hated them, as though trying to flick them off. 'My hands,' she screamed. 'It's sticky on my hands. It's slimy. Do something, Max. Max, do something please. I've got cyanide on my hands. I've wiped it on my clothes. It's on my shoes. I've been standing in it. Max, it's all over the road.' Her voice had become a gabble, sentences running one over the other, not properly formed.

SEVEN

Underneath

A VOICE WAS calling her. It must have been time to get up but Alison knew it was dark and she didn't want to get up while it was dark. The dormitory light wasn't on. It wasn't fair of Mrs Cartwright to call her before the lights went on. But the call was different and the bed was different; it was lumpy and cold and terribly tight. The call wasn't saying, 'Come on, girls; time to get up.' It was saying, 'Alison,' over and over again, as though the word itself was an ache. Then the call went away for a time, perhaps to wake someone else.

'Alison.'

It was not Mrs Cartwright; the voice was different; almost but not quite a man's. It almost cried, but didn't. It floated like a piece of paper on water slowly turning round. Her name was written on it and she saw it only by glimpses. The rest of the time it was upside down, or on edge, or too far away.

'Alison.'

It was a voice again. It was a man's. It was Dad's.

'Yes,' she said, 'I'm coming. Things are in a tangle here.' She couldn't get out of bed.

'Alison, love.'

'All right, Dad. Just a tick. I'll be there.'

She tried to struggle out through blankets and sheets that held her like a captive wound in a sack.

'Alison!' His voice was a little unusual, as though the effort of producing it called deeply on his strength. (She was faintly aware of that.) 'Don't fight. Stay still. You'll hurt yourself.'

She didn't understand, not even then, because she had been so certain she was asleep in bed.

'We're over the edge, love. The cabin's crushed.'

Then the sounds came back; sounds like rolling thunders and breaking waves and distant gunfire. And sensations came back; thuddings and wrenchings in her neck, and a rearing-up as though she had ridden a horse hard to the end of its tether.

She was suddenly sick.

'Are you all right?'

He asked twice, but she couldn't answer. All she could do was groan for breath and plead for the contractions in her stomach to stop. She couldn't even find her arms to help herself; they were there all right, they weren't broken, but they wouldn't come free or didn't want to come free. They seemed to have a will of their own.

She fought with herself for a while, trying to control all the functions that wanted to go wrong; legs that wanted to kick, hands that wanted to claw, eyes that wanted to dilate, a voice that wanted to scream. Her body seemed to be full of devils trying to break out. 'Look what you've done to me,' every part of her wanted to shout, 'you've smashed me up, all because you wouldn't wait. Call yourself a father . . .'

Then the storm began to wash out, to ease away, and utter exhaustion took its place.

Dad said, 'Are you all right, love? Is anything broken?'

After a pause, he said, 'Are you bleeding?'

A little later, he said, 'Does your head hurt? Is your back all right?'

But she couldn't answer him, not then. She wanted nothing more than to lie quiet. Questions were not for answering; they were only for listening to. They were like voices in another room that were not her concern. Everything was so dark, so black, so crowded. Unidentifiable masses of metal hemmed her about. Tentatively, she began to push in different directions, with her shoulders, her knees, her hips, but nothing gave an inch. She could have been nailed into a coffin. She was sick again.

Dad said, 'Easy, love, easy . . .'

Then he said, 'Alison; I've got to know if you're all right.'

But she wouldn't answer him. For a while she had hated him with violence; now she was indifferent not only to what he said, but to *him*. He could stew in his own juice; he could say what he liked; she didn't care if he was broken in every limb—it would serve him right!

'Dad,' she cried suddenly, bursting out, 'you're not hurt?'

There was faint surprise in his strained voice. 'I could be worse, love. Could be dead, I guess. What of you?'

'I think I'm all right but I don't really know. I can't— I can't—'

'You can't *what*?'

'I can't get my hands out. They seem to be stuck; they seem to be tied there with ropes.'

'Are they?' It was a deliberately casual tone and she knew what each question was going to be before he put it into words. 'Your finger-tips, love. Have you got nerves there?'

'Yes, Dad.'

'What about your toes and your head? Have you got movement?'

'I know they're all right, Dad. It's not my spine, really it's not.'

'Who said anything about your spine?'

'Oh, Dad, I know what you mean. I know. Maybe I'm just trapped.'

'You've got to be hurt somewhere, love. You couldn't have got out of it scot-free.'

'I didn't say I had done, but my belt's not broken. I can still feel it there.'

'What about breathing? Does it hurt to breathe?'

'No, it's got nothing to do with that either.'

She heard his sigh, long and low. 'There's not too much

wrong with you, thank God. You must be able to move in some direction, surely?'

'I can push but it doesn't get me anywhere. I seem to be in a *tunnel*.'

'Perhaps you are,' he said, 'a tunnel of sorts. The cabin's like a sandwich, crushed flat . . . Oh, Alison, Alison.'

She wondered where he was; in what position he was lying. His voice sounded metallic as though issuing from an old-fashioned radio set. It was impossible to know whether he was above her or below or away to one side. It was an awful struggle not to shrill like a frightened child of eight or nine. 'Dad! Will we ever get out?'

'Of course we will. It'll be daylight in a few hours and then someone will come.'

'Who?'

'Someone, someone.'

'We haven't seen a house in miles.'

'There are people about,' he said, in an odd sort of tone that implied that he knew.

'It's terribly cold, Dad. Do you think we'll freeze?'

'Better than the other way around. We could have burnt.' But he hurried over that. 'We're wrong side up I think; probably with the trailer on top.' His voice broke again. 'I'm terribly sorry, love.'

Alison whimpered under her breath, desperately wishing to wake up from an evil dream. These things never happened to you; never, never happened to you. 'You didn't mean to do it, Dad. You couldn't help it. It was only bad luck.'

The metallic voice was silent, passing that over. Perhaps her choice of words had hurt him, though she had not intended that it should. 'You *are* all right, aren't you, Dad?'

For a while she thought he was not going to answer that either. 'Fair enough, love.'

It was a strange conversation, as though between dis-embodied voices in a tomb. There was a giddiness in it, as though gravity had relaxed its pull. And now there were lies in it. He was hurt. He might even be bleeding to death. How could she tell?

She heard him again, that voice in space: 'I was hoping

you'd be able to get out, to go for help, because there are problems, love. Awful problems. Awful.'

She didn't understand; it was not an easy statement to sort out.

But he went on, as though addressing her across a wide open place, forming his words theatrically, more and more distinctly as he went, as though he took a peculiar delight in inflicting deeper wounds upon himself, as though each word was a challenge he had to face, as though the framing of it was an exhausting feat of strength. He frightened her until it was all she could do not to cry out. 'It's our load, love. There was enough poison on the back to wipe out half the State. Cyanides of different kinds; other chemicals, too; awful, deadly stuff. Takes only a few grains to kill a man. You can't roll a transport like this and leave the load intact. Where's it ended up? I heard it go, thudding off downhill. Thirty-eight drums of poison, love. There's a dam down there; and people must drink. What am I going to do; how am I to get out of the cab before people start falling dead?'

'You couldn't help it! It was not your fault!'

There was silence again, and coldness, and dampness, and smell.

'We've got problems, love. You've got to get out.'

'I can't, I can't; can't you?'

'Me, they've got to cut out with a hacksaw or an acetylene torch. Then maybe they'll lay me out. My just deserts.'

'*Dad.*'

'It's my fault. It's not "one of those things". It's not just rotten bad luck.'

'What are you saying, Dad? Of course it's not your fault.'

'We jack-knifed on the curve. My fault. We dragged the trailer behind us at right angles to the road. I'm not a mug, love. I've sat at wheels like this one, what's left of it, for sixteen years. But tonight I jack-knifed, and I can't forgive myself for that. I shouldn't have been on the road at all. And what have I done to you? What have I done to them?'

'Them? No one's drunk the water yet. Anyway, the water

might be all right. It was an accident, Dad. You know it was. Why are you doing this to yourself?'

'You've got to go for help.'

'I *can't* get out. I've tried and tried. I don't want to make myself sick again.'

'I saw a trailer jack-knife once, on the coastal road. Fellow came round a curve with his trailer at right angles to the road. Wet road, slippery like this one. He didn't know; he didn't know. If it hadn't straightened up like a whip-crack he'd have cut me in two. I just sat at the wheel and froze, with the sea on my left hand at the foot of the cliffs and this fellow coming at me on the right. Helpless. Until it straightened up like a whip-crack. And he didn't know. He never knew.'

'Please, please, Dad. I don't know why you're talking like this.'

'We had our trailer, love, at right-angles to the road. We must have done or they would have seen the lights. They should've seen the lights; they should've seen them. They accelerated out of the bend and rammed us. Crazy, but it's what they did. They ran underneath. I felt them hit. I saw them hit. I saw the mirror flash, saw them out of the back of my head. We took them over the edge. That's where they are now, under us, or on top, or somewhere about. We've got problems, love. We've got problems.'

When she started on him, hysterically blaming *them*, he didn't hear her, any more than she knew what she said.

Then it was quiet in the cab, and cold, and black.

EIGHT

David Come Back

THE DOOR BEHIND Tony gave way without warning, a complete surprise, and he sprawled on his back into David's room as David knew he would. David couldn't see what had happened, but he heard the thud and Tony's startled shout and each amused him as much as the other. He stood in the dark, invisible, chuckling to himself.

David loved thuds and sudden noises like slamming doors. Sometimes (when he was quick and dodged all the grabbing hands) he lifted the end of the dining-table set for a meal and crashed it down. He laughed then until tears were in his eyes. He loved shouts and cries and clowns. At the circus he shrieked with delight every time the clown fell over, and the clown, wise man, with a heart beneath his paint, played for David that day as he played for no other.

David remembered the clown and loved him, because nothing happened of that kind—the good or the bad—that David forgot. He remembered the clown when Tony fell into his room and he went to the circus again in his mind. The clown gave him a flower, climbing the tiers to place it in his hand, and David kept it until one day he couldn't find it any more. He cried and cried but the flower had gone away and no other flower would do. Now, remembering it, he stopped laughing and began to cry. He still looked for the flower at times, everywhere in his room, that other room a long time away before they got in the car and came.

He looked under the bed and on the window-sill and in the plastic basket where he kept his treasures—torn paper, pages from cardboard books, plastic skittles, rubber rabbits, soft wheels that belonged to broken things. Sometimes he just stretched on the floor, kicking his heels, thinking of his flower, trying to say the word so that someone would know, but it wasn't a word that he could form. Flower, why did you go away? Where did you go?

Tony's fumbling hands found him in the dark and lifted him on to the bed with a terrific grunt. Hands were always finding David, lifting him up or pulling him back or putting him down. Then Tony sat on the bed beside him, cuddling up close (cold, cold Tony, like water at the beach), talking, talking the way everyone talked when they talked to David, saying the same things over like a clock. 'Gee, Fatso, I wonder what, Mum and Dad are awful late. Mum and Dad haven't come back. Gee, Fatso, you're lovely and hot.'

Tick tock. Tick tock.

'How can you be so hot when it's so cold everywhere else? I'm glad you opened up. I thought you never would. I didn't mind the bump. Why are Mum and Dad so late?'

Tick tock. Tick tock.

'Let's lie down, Fatso. Let's try to sleep. I don't want to stay awake. What do you say, Fatso? Let's try to go to sleep.'

Tick tock. Tick tock.

Tony dragged the bedclothes over, wrenching them from underneath, but David wouldn't lie down because it was time to be up. Tony pulled him down and David sat up. 'Please, Fatso, let's go to sleep.'

Tony pulled him down again, but David sat up.

'Horse feathers! I want to go to sleep. I don't want to stay awake.'

It was a game and David put his head down, then leapt up, and put it down again. 'Bang, bang,' laughed David, 'I love banging up and banging down. You bang as well.' But it didn't sound like that and Tony didn't know what he said.

'Fatso,' Tony cried, 'please, please go to sleep. I just don't want to stay awake.'

They *never* knew what David said. It was easier to talk to cats than to people in the house. 'Say this,' people said, 'or say that,' but when he said it they sighed, 'You can't expect it of him, poor kid.' '*I said it; I said it.*' But they always smiled and went on with something else. He'd dance round them and say, 'I said it; I said it.' But they wouldn't even look up—only Tony did sometimes. 'I'm sorry, Fatso,' Tony sometimes said, 'it doesn't make sense.' It was easier talking to cats, except that they scratched.

Then, because David was sitting up straight and his ears were not buried under blankets, he heard the car outside somewhere close. 'Tony,' he said, 'they've come. Now can I get up?'

'Go to sleep, pest.'

Then slowly Tony, also, sat up, not because he grasped a word of David's statement, but because he heard the engine for himself, sensed the headlights nosing through the fog, almost saw his father's eyes peering out.

'Mum and Dad,' he breathed, 'they're back. They're all right.' It was the strangest feeling, like winning a race when you'd expected to come last. It was like all his inside being folded into knots and drawn tight.

'I'll get up now,' David said. 'I'll kick the wall.'

But it was not a language that Tony understood, and suddenly Tony felt a fool, he was suddenly afraid that they might find him skulking like a baby in David's bed; he suddenly remembered the wide-open door and the house full of fog. 'Crumbs,' he said, and scooted out of bed, missing (unseen) the sharp edge of the bedroom door by an inch at the most, flinching instinctively from it with a yelp, waving his arms through the living-room. 'Shoo, fog; shoo, shoo, shoo!' He tried to drive it out, slamming the outside door, but now stumbling into things, tumbling over a chair, yelping again, hissing like a punctured tyre through his teeth, while David, delighted beyond belief that Tony was ready for fun in the dark, shrieked with laughter and bounced on his bed-springs until they creaked like a rusty cart.

'Shut up,' Tony yelled, 'you'll give the game away.'

'Game,' shrilled David, and bounced higher.

'Shut up,' Tony yelled, 'oh, my gosh . . .' And groped into his own bed with hardly a breath left.

'David,' he screeched, 'stop it, stop it. If you don't stop I'll thump you on the head.'

David stopped. *Thump* was a word that could mean painful things. It could mean a game, but not when there was anger in the voice. After the clown fell over he climbed the tiers and gave David a flower; after Tony fell over he screeched with anger through the wall.

There wasn't a car now, not even the murmur of the engine that Tony had expected under the house. No slamming doors that meant *people* were home. No laughter from Brenda or Max trying to explain the fears that had sent them up the hill. For curious seconds that dragged and dragged it was quiet out there until something thudded unexpectedly against the ramp.

Tony sat upright. There were footsteps; but not footsteps that he knew. Then a voice called, 'Are you there, Mrs Shaw?' Then a knocking started, not sharp with the knuckles, but heavy with the edge of the hand.

'Are you there? Are you all right there? *Mrs Shaw!*'

It was a man's voice, a vaguely familiar voice, distorted by walls and glass and fog and the panic in Tony's heart. It was not Mum and Dad. It was not Brenda nor Max.

Tony couldn't stop himself.

The cry welled up from deep down, shaking him with sobs, flooding his eyes with tears.

'Who's crying in there? What's going on in there? Open up. Mrs Shaw, Mrs Shaw, it's Fenwick here!'

David cried because Tony cried.

'Will someone open the door!'

The knocking changed. It was not the sort of knocking a hand could have made. To Tony it sounded as he imagined a battering ram would, but he couldn't answer because he was crying uncontrollably for Mum and Dad, and because big boys of eleven don't cry when strangers are around.

The outside door crashed open with a splitting of wood

and the beam of a torch flashed in. 'All right, you people, whoever you are. I've got a gun.'

Max had barely grasped what Brenda said about cyanide before her words became a gabble. She was like a person possessed, not responsible for her thoughts or actions, and in all honesty he took no conscious aim. He let go with his right hand held flat before he knew it, throwing a frantic swing into the dark to silence her, then trying to pull it back because brothers didn't hit sisters with mighty blows like that. He missed her, but caught her hair with his finger-tips, wrenching it, stinging her with the shock.

'Stand as you are,' he hissed, with a terrible calmness that was nothing like the emotion he felt.

Her gabble became a sobbing sound, a gulping for breath, turning into another kind of horror, a horror almost of herself.

'It's on the outside of you, sis. You know darned well you haven't swallowed the stuff.'

But she couldn't speak, because she could feel it stabbing at her inside, like red-hot arrows thrusting in her chest. It wasn't there, she knew it wasn't there, but the dread of it was as real as any fear she had ever felt. 'What'll I do?' an inner voice kept saying, 'how am I to get it off?' And in Max a voice was saying, 'What'll I do with her? How will I get it off? What are the properties of cyanide? Will it hurt being on the skin? Does it hurt to breathe the fumes in? Will it wash off? What do you neutralize it with? Is it acid or alkali or what?'

Out loud Max said, as though nothing could disturb his calm, 'Now quieten down. There's nothing to worry about. It's nothing that water won't shift.'

'But there's no water here!'

'Then we'll get some. There's the spring at the hairpin bend. We'll go there and then you can wash it off.' It was simple enough, sensible enough. He hadn't thought of it until the words came out.

'But it's on my clothes and shoes and all over the road.'

'What of it? We'll brush it off. People who work with the

stuff must get it on their clothes and hands and shoes every day of the week. If it'll wash off for them it'll wash off for us.' He convinced even himself. 'It's not like caustic or acid. It's not going to burn holes in you.'

She was still panting, still swallowing air after every few words. 'Do you really know or are you making it up?'

'Photographers use it,' he said, 'or they used to, in the old wet-plate process. It's in that book of Dad's. Crikey, sis, you know that.'

'I know they use it to kill rats!' But the panic had gone, leaving her wrung out. The panic couldn't go on, not while this calmness flowed from Max. 'How do we get to the spring?' she said, 'without the torch?'

The torch was lying where she had thrown it, still active, still draining light on the road.

'Why should we be without it?'

'Don't touch it, Max!'

'Why?'

'The stuff's on my hands. It's on the torch.'

'If it'll wash off you, it'll wash off me, and I guess it'll wash off the torch.'

He picked it up, turning his face away from Brenda, setting his jaws and teeth, half-expecting it to bite, almost certain that it would sting. But nothing happened. It wasn't raw to the touch, or slimy, or anything but itself.

'Come on, sis,' he said.

She trailed after him weakly, like clay at the knees.

'Don't wipe your hands on your clothes again, sis; let's keep it as simple as we can.'

'Golly, Max . . .' But she said nothing more; she let slide all the things she felt she should have said. They wouldn't come out right; they might only start another row, the way all rows happened, out of nothing for no reason that anyone could remember; but beating back into her brain were the words: 'It's not Mum and Dad; it's a truck. It's not Mum and Dad; it's a truck.' Even cyanide, horrible, slimy stuff, was better than that awful, empty gulf.

Max stopped and immediately she stopped also, hands

held away from her clothes, while she trembled from head to foot.

'What's up?'

He moved the torch beam like an extension of his own arm. 'There!' In the light was another drum, against the bank, in the ditch. 'Potassium cyanide; same as the other; but it's not broken.' Max shuddered; to him it looked like an unexploded bomb. 'That makes two. What would Dad want with two drums? Less, I guess, than he'd want with one. You must have been right, sis; it was a truck.'

There was a bleakness in him that was neither relief nor concern. He was struggling with himself, trying to think *right* when all his instincts ran the other way. He *knew* there was an accident, a terrible one, and it was not right to feel relief for any reason at all, yet for an unknown truck (not a human thing) that had spilled poison far and wide he could not feel sadness. It was bad, very bad, of that truck to scatter poison on the road. But where were Mum and Dad?

Brenda's heart was fluttering like a leaf. 'Come on, Max. Forget the old drum. Get me to the spring.'

'Yeh,' he said, and had to drag the light away and walk on, uphill.

'How far is it, Max?'

'I don't know. Not far. Hard to say. Stick to the ditch and we'll get there.'

'I want to get it off, Max.'

'Yeh, yeh. I know.'

'What am I going to do where it's on my clothes? I don't mean later; I mean now! I can't wash my clothes. I can't take them off. It's too cold to stand round without clothes on.'

'Look, we've covered this before, sis. We'll get your hands clean and get you back to the house. Stop panicking. It'll work out.'

She stumbled after him, trying to keep up. He was striding it out, almost blindly, steering a course at the edge of the ditch.

'Wouldn't it be better to go back that way now, Max,

to get to the spring where it comes out lower down? I think I'd rather go down. We know where the spring is down there. There are lots of springs down there, Max.'

'Will you stop panicking!'

'It's all right for you; you haven't got it on you. Up this way we don't know how far it is.'

'It's *not* far,' he said irritably. 'We've been walking uphill for half an hour. More than that. Forty-five minutes we've been walking. We must be nearly there and we've got to go this way. Haven't we? We've got to know what it's all about.'

'We know enough already. A truck lost its load. What more do we want to know? Please, Max, please; let's go back.'

He didn't stop.

'You're going too fast. Wait on, wait on.' She stumbled after him; it was like a dream. 'Wait for me, Max. What are you trying to do?'

He didn't know. His body was moving mechanically, but not smoothly. Fog was in his lungs, in his joints, grating like sand.

'Look, Max, the torch will be flat if we don't go back. It's such a stupid little torch. It only lasts a few minutes, Max. We'll be stranded in the dark if we don't go back.'

'Oh, get a grip on yourself . . .' Then he stopped suddenly, with a sharp intake of breath that hurt in his throat, with a stop so sudden that he almost overbalanced.

Drums were strewn on the road, one of them broken. Two, three, *four* broken as the shaking torch beam found them one after the other. Marbles of potassium cyanide, chipped-off flakes and dust of it lay everywhere pungently poisoning the air; and a red spill from rectangular containers of a different kind looked horribly evil, looked horribly lethal, looked like armies of red-back spiders massing on the ground.

Brenda sobbed, 'I don't want to stay, Max. I don't want to know. *I don't want to stay, Max.* Take me back to the house.'

He didn't really hear her because her hands had fastened on him and were pulling at him and he was repulsed by her touch. 'Take your hands off me,' he shrilled, wrenching himself free. 'I don't want it on me, too.'

Brenda saw him break away into the dark, like a shadow passing across her eyes, away from the cyanide, downhill, and she ran after him crying for him to wait.

Light moved across doorways and over walls and Tony almost choked himself trying to be quiet. The man had said, 'I've got a gun. I've got a gun. I've got a gun . . .' He had said it only once but it went round and round in a sudden questioning silence full of a different kind of fright that turned little sounds into big shuddering noises; heart-beats drummed, even tears dripped audibly to the sheets. David stopped crying, suddenly, as only David could. Even the man who had smashed the door open changed from something solid into the far-away man he was at other times.

Mr Fenwick didn't like kids. He went fishing in his boat and never took kids. He had a black beard that Mum said needed a trim. He worked with his wife on television and they had tickets on themselves as big as roadside hoardings, Max said. Their shack was a mile round the lake and thank heaven it wasn't any closer, Dad said. What was Mr Fenwick doing with a gun?

The light moved back and forth, then went out.

There were shuffling sounds, and a stage whisper, 'I said I've got a gun. It's a rifle. It's a repeater. I won't miss.'

After a while the whisper went on, 'I know there's trouble here. Don't make it worse. Don't make me nervous. I might shoot.'

Suddenly, Tony wailed, 'I'm here, Mr Fenwick. In my room.' And David's bed creaked.

'*Who's that?*' The voice was sharp.

'Tony! It's Tony, Mr Fenwick, and David. Only us. Don't shoot. Please don't shoot.'

'Who's with you? What's going on? Where's your mother? Where are your brother and sister? What's happened to them?' The questions came rapidly, breathlessly.

'There's no one else here, Mr Fenwick. Only us. Only David and me.'

'I don't believe it. You wouldn't be left like this.'

'Really, Mr Fenwick. Really and truly. There's no one else.'

After a pause the voice came less breathlessly. 'Why is the house dark?'

'Because it's night time, Mr Fenwick.'

Tony wished he would go away. He was so frightened, and underneath his fright was a misery as black as a pit.

'Come on out, Tony. Show yourself. I'm not happy about this.'

'Don't shoot, Mr Fenwick.'

'Of course I won't shoot. Come on. Come on out.'

Tony sobbed. 'I don't want to come out.'

He heard the man sigh heavily, apparently very close, then the door to Tony's room cracked open and bright light dazzled him. Next door, from the next room, David cried out.

As suddenly as light had flooded in on Tony it was gone, apparently to flood in on David because another door crashed against the wall as Tony's had done, then after that in succession door after door crashed and Tony was too scared to move, too scared to think. He couldn't understand the violence of it, the brute force of the man, the crash, crash, crash of doors, or the gun, the rifle, the repeater that wouldn't miss. Then there was silence again, nothing except that stunned sensation in Tony's head; noises happening in his nerve-ends but not happening in fact. Switches started clicking on and off; floorboards groaned.

The light came back, and the voice with it, sounding surprised, sounding almost relieved. 'Tony; where *is* the rest of your family?

'Tony; what are you doing here by yourselves in an empty house?

'Why were you crying?

'Were you frightened because you were on your own in the dark?

'Come on, Tony, answer me.

'Look, lad, I'm sorry if I frightened you, but I didn't know what to think. Some noises woke my wife. She wondered if they were shots. Something's happened, Tony, hasn't it? I only came to see if everything was all right. I can't help you, Tony, unless you tell me.

'It could have been murder. These things happen. A family in an isolated place without a man. It can happen. Awful things can happen. That's what my wife said. That's why I came.'

But Tony sat speechless, with his eyes closed against the glare of the lantern.

'My wife's an actress, Tony. That's why she thinks these things. She has a very active imagination. I don't know yet whether she's right or wrong. I won't know until you tell me.

'What are you doing fully dressed at this hour of the night? You don't always wear your shoes to bed; I'm sure you don't. It's after three. It's very late. I should have come long ago; I know that now. I thought about it for too long.'

A heavy weight bore on the bed and a hand touched Tony's shoulder. 'I'm sorry, Tony. I didn't mean to frighten you. I'm not the sort of man who goes round frightening little boys. But what was I to think when I heard you crying? I thought perhaps I'd have a couple of thugs to fight; I thought I might find people dead. Because I haven't got a gun at all, you see. Only a piece of wood. What's wrong, Tony? Come on, lad, tell me.'

The hand crept farther round Tony's shoulder and the arm began to bear against him. It was a thicker arm than Dad's. It was very strong and Tony buried his face into the fabric of the man's coat. 'Come on, Tony lad. What's the trouble? Tell me about it.'

Then it came, pouring out, in a confusion of sobs and half-finished sentences, all of it, all about the accident that had happened somewhere on the hill, all about Max and Brenda, all about David and Tony on their own, all about the candle going out, all about Mum and Dad, all about Sid Gore with black holes for eyes. And the arm about him never relaxed, held on to him tightly all the time, even after there was nothing more to say, even after everything was out, everything was gone, and silence came back.

Nothing happened, only quiet, only the unvarying

pressure of the arm, only the man's warm breath striking against Tony's neck. Then there was a feeling of calm, of having found somewhere safe.

'All right, Tony,' he said, 'you can both get in the car. You'll be better there than here. Then we'll drive up the hill and take a look. Would you like to do that?'

Tony sniffed into the man's coat.

'Rug up your brother David; he'll catch cold the way he's dressed.'

'David never gets cold. David's always beaut and hot.'

'He's a lucky boy, then, isn't he? But rug him up, nevertheless.'

The strong arms straightened Tony up. 'Wipe your eyes. Come on. Wipe up the mess. I can't stand snotty-nosed kids.' But there was a kindness in the way that he said it. Tony didn't take offence. He groped for the sheet and pressed it against his face.

'It's not often that things are as bad as they look. Once you're up and doing you might be surprised how they sort themselves out.'

But Tony didn't want to move. It was much too safe where he was to run the risk of anything else. 'Do you think it *is* an accident, Mr Fenwick?'

'I don't know, lad. It was my wife who heard it and she thought it was shots. I was sound asleep.'

'But Mum and Dad are so late.'

'Yes; they are; but they could have had a puncture or a breakdown. Even the train might have been late. It's a very soupy sort of night. Not a night for driving far. Not a night for being out. Up you get. Fix up David; you'll know where his clothes are kept. Then we'll be off.'

Tony didn't want to move but the strong arms drew him from the bed and planted him on his feet. The lantern was on the floor, shining straight up, diffusing its beam against the ceiling. He felt a bit giddy, weaving round it, to reach his overcoat tossed across a chair.

The position of the lantern changed; it was in Mr Fenwick's hand now and everything in the house, even things Tony couldn't see, seemed to lean and sway and then return. He felt weak. A hand took his arm and guided him into David's room. David wasn't there.

'Hey, Fatso,' Tony said. 'Car. Car. Ride in a car. Come on, Fatso. Don't muck about.'

David wasn't under the bed or behind the curtain. He wasn't there.

The lantern went away, leaving Tony in the dark. 'He's not out here,' Mr Fenwick said. 'Where are you, David? Don't hide. No one's going to hurt you. Tony; does he understand when you talk to him?'

Deep inside Tony something nasty stirred, a feeling that hurried him into the living-room, that ridiculous room lined like a railway carriage with doors, a feeling that made him take the lantern from Mr Fenwick's hand, that drove him from one bedroom to another, to all the cupboards, all the corners, all the places where David sometimes hid as silently as a cat, smiling.

'Fatso,' he shrieked. 'Where are you?'

Behind him Tony sensed the man, a pace or two behind all the time; but sometimes in front of him like a stranger in a crowd. Then, suddenly, he turned, a stranger with a frown confronting something he didn't understand.

'He's not here,' Tony said, trembling. 'You frightened him.'

'Of course he's here.'

Tony turned the lantern on the outside door, splintered at the lock, with nails and screws exposed.

'He's gone,' Tony said.

'Of course he's not gone. No child would go out there.'

'He's gone! You don't understand. No one else ever understands. You mustn't leave doors open. You mustn't ever leave them unlocked. You didn't even latch his bedroom door. Fatso's gone.

'Fatso! Fatso!'

Tony fled to the outside door.

'David,' he wailed, 'David come back. You'll fall in the dam.'

Tony blundered out into the night, into the fog, slipping wildly on the ramp, bellowing at the top of his voice. 'No, no, no. You mustn't go away. I'm looking after you. You mustn't go away.'

NINE

Voice in Another Room

FOR A TIME it was as though death had come to the crushed cabin. It was as soundless as the hillside, as motionless as if it had become a rock that had rested there a thousand years. Silently it added to frost and fog and bush odours strange properties of its own, smells of oil, smells of rubber, smells of battery acid, smells of dust now dislodged but gathered fragment by fragment from ninety thousand miles of road.

No one came.

'Dad . . .'

Her call was like a faint signal of uncertain authority that did not expect an answer, almost as if she addressed herself. 'Are we in trouble because the car hit us? If they're dead . . .?'

Breaking the silence, even with a whisper, was like shouting in church, but the silence that had been there before dragged on, as though lofty, vaulted ceilings that did not exist absorbed her breath. Minutes lay still but somewhere his words were in them like thoughts on a wavelength that could be heard. It was eerie, and she was afraid of it; as though it belonged to a state of existence outside life.

'Mightn't be "they", might it? Might only be one.'

She didn't know when he said it; it could have come immediately or later by an age.

'Might have been a car full of kids. Usually is a car full

of kids. They kill themselves as though they didn't care. As though it was fun. Who'd come hell-bent out of a bend except a carload of kids?'

She knew he said it but didn't know when.

'Twenty-five years I've had my licence and never hit a dog. It's the car behind that's got to do the stopping in time to save itself. No problems with the Law; just problems with myself.'

She began to dislike less the silence with the words floating in it. It was outside life and couldn't hurt. It was like listening to a story about someone else when you were not awake. Then there wasn't any story. Only something like sleep with words in it that didn't add up.

'You're not hurt. It's only shock. Think warm like you're in a hot bath.'

'You won't be penniless. There's insurance and things like that.'

'Keep on at school. Take all of it you can get. School's a good place for kids when they're growing up. We don't want another ignoramus in the family who can't pick a winner on the track.'

'They're dead, or we would have heard. There'd have been a move by now. There'd have been a noise. They'd have called or come to help. Could it be them? From Finn's? What a twist of fate?'

'Think warm like you're in a hot bath, steam on the mirror, steam on the ceiling. Have a good soak.'

'If I've disappointed you, love, I'm sorry. But it can't be helped. Some day you had to see through the bluff. The Uncle Ted bit didn't help. Or was it Fred? I guess *Finn's Folly*'s not really on the map. But *this* one, of all the roads we had to pick.'

'Men are only men. Poor old Fred. He spins a yarn in a pub and does his mate in. He never meant me to come. I never meant to come myself. I don't know what I meant.'

'You kids expect too much. Don't hate me, love, for the things I'm not. Your friends for wanting fathers that are playmates; you for wanting one that's a toff.'

She heard it, but he could have said it first, or last, or

thought it aloud to himself. Or she could have invented it without his help.

'When I was your age I was going to do a lot.'

'I've done nothing much, except fool about.'

'I was going to learn the fiddle. Can't play a note.'

'Never read a decent book.'

'Never made a garden.'

'Never planted a tree. Everyone should plant a tree, at least once.'

'Never had a good fight; always chickened out.'

'Never gone to church except with your mother to be wed. You haven't been christened, love. Never got round to it. I don't suppose it matters much.'

'Your mother's not dead, love. You should know that, if you've never guessed.'

'Turn on the tap. Top up the bath. Don't get cold, love. Think hot.'

'She just packed up and went off. She went interstate.'

'A bit like yourself. Too big for her boots, though she made them fit. A girl who knew what she wanted to get. She was a doll, but as cold as a fish. She's wiser now, I guess.'

'I don't know what to do about this. It's too difficult for me. Do you want me to tell you who she is? It's not the name she was born with. It's one of several she made up herself.'

He said that, too, sometime or other. Perhaps it was then or years ago when she was little. She tried to say 'yes' but the word wouldn't come out.

'If we'd had a family, grandmas and uncles and aunts and people like that, you'd have been told before this. It would have come out in the wash. You've seen her, love, once or twice. She's what you might call a face. You can see it and you can hear it but you can't touch. No maternal instinct. As cold as a fish.'

'I can't even die clean. Got to dirty up the place with a carload of kids and cyanide all over the joint.'

'Keep the bath hot, love. Think hot.'

'It's cold in the fog.'

Perhaps he said it. Perhaps not. It was only a silence with words floating in it.

TEN

The Opalescent Cloud

MAX RAN DOWN that awful hill, away from the place where the poisons were, through that fog, until an instinct warned him he was a moment short of stumbling off the edge. He stopped, yet had to resist an urge to go on, to stumble the extra stride that would pitch him into scrub on to a rock-strewn slope where he knew he would be unable to stand, where he would roll, where he would tumble, crack his head, break a leg. Something in him longed to fall, to suffer injury, to be hurt beyond the point where accidents and poisons and Brenda and Mum and Dad would worry him any more. He wanted to be out of it, to be somewhere else, never to have heard. He wanted this night to live over again, asleep in bed, undisturbed.

He drooped on the road, with an awful ache in his thin body, head bowed, the palm of one hand pressed to his eyes, flinching from Brenda's presence that bore against him like despair.

'I'm sorry,' he panted, but didn't turn to her. 'I know I'm a rat. I hate myself, Brenda.'

But she kept her hands off and somehow had the wisdom not to snap or snarl. In a way she understood. In a way she knew.

'You take the torch,' he said, trying to talk sense, trying to find his self-command. 'Go down to where the spring comes out. Give yourself a good wash to get the cyanide off, then go on home. Drop your clothes in the carport. Change into something else. Get back as soon as you can. I'll wait.'

'Don't make me go alone,' she said, 'please, Max, not all that way.'

'You've got to, and I've got to stay here. I can't run away. Golly, sis, I want to run away; but I can't. If Mum and Dad are here and I run away . . .'

He felt her hand touch his own, felt the torch go, and suddenly, in an extraordinary way, felt free, felt warm, felt the lifting of an awful weight.

He was alone and didn't have to act a part any longer. With Brenda he always had to act a part simply to hold his own. With Tony he always had to act a part because Tony thought he was a hero. Even with David. It was a different part for everybody. But the boy who was really Max was hidden deep down; being alone was marvellous; no acting, no poses, no worrying about what others would think.

He sank to his haunches, sat on the road, and sadness flowed over him. It wasn't ugly, it wasn't frightening, but it was strange. Strangest of all was the feeling that sadness filled the world, that it was always there like music continually playing, waiting to be heard, that facing up to death was part of living and better than running away.

The hillside came back (for a while it had withdrawn) intruding upon him with its fog, its cold, its dampness and its mysteries. Brenda had gone; there was no sound that did not belong to trees or earth. The faintly luminous hands of his watch showed half-past three.

Mum and Dad were an hour and thirty minutes late. They would not be coming now.

He struggled to his feet against the stiffness of the cold and the wet, still deep in his sadness but not disabled by it.

There was poison on the hill; it had to be moved.

There was an accident; it had to be found.

There were people, probably dead, or they would have made sounds.

But there was a fog, an opalescent cloud lit only by a moon that could not break through.

He walked back uphill, slowly, stiffly, determined not to turn away again, determined to hold his mood of sadness that made feelings like fear and fright and horror seem shallow and out of place. (Vaguely he wondered if this were another pose?) Sadness was like an armour that he could wear against the threat of lesser things, but he kept clear of the ditch because that was where the poisons lay and groped up the outside edge, peering at his feet, using his hands as a guard for his head against twigs and leaves; suddenly, after a while, glimpsing his watch with surprise. He had walked for minutes on the road.

Then he stepped through cyanide, heard it crush, felt it slip, felt marbles through the soles of his shoes, felt one eject from the side like a shot from a sling, to bounce away. It sickened him almost to the soul and with a gasp he leapt clear only to land in more. Marbles of slime clinked against each other (a nightmare thought: 'I'll fall') and everywhere the smell was sweet in a horrid way. He tried to stop breathing, tried to be calm, tried to shuffle out of it with his feet flat to the road but ran into a ridge fully twelve inches high.

Max swallowed painfully (something *stung* in his throat), all sadness gone. It was different now; a frozen, appalled feeling. A ridge of cyanide a foot high missed when he had walked up with Brenda because they had walked on the inside; missed even on his mad rush away. Or had he reached a point higher than before? It was against his shoes, he could feel it against his toes, like a man-trap.

Max didn't move.

With his sleeve he wiped beads of fog from his eyelashes, wiped them from his nose; tried desperately to see. Something was odd; it was not the same. It was gravel and mud down there in the ridge, not cyanide at all. Something closed about his spine. He strained to see, rubbing his eyes. Was there a score-mark in the road, a furrow almost as though ploughed?

Everything turned cold, even the warmth left inside him turned over like a page, from blood to ice.

'Please, God,' he said, 'I know what I've found.'

It rose up then against every wish and prayer that struggled to keep it down, a weak cry that no one more than yards away could have heard. 'Mum. Dad. Am I standing where you died?'

Over the edge; somewhere down there.

Branches, faintly seen, hung like tattered clothes, leaves littered the road. Other things were there, perceived laboriously in the gloom one at a time, his brain seeing them and identifying them rather than his eyes; strips of wood with bolts torn through, glass fractured like cheap beads, sheet-metal ripped like cardboard, drums, canisters, rope, crates, cloth, angle-iron, one twisted wheel and slashed pieces of tyre.

The edge of the road was broken away, scooped, as though a steam shovel had run wild.

Max couldn't move. He stood in the midst of it, leaning against waves of sadness coming back again, vaguely remembering the ruins of disasters seen on television screens, ruins of earthquake, fire, flood, aeroplanes, railway trains, war. But they were not the same. Ruins on a television screen were two feet square, contained in a cathode ray tube. They were locked in, caged. Then the picture would change and instantly they were gone and the announcer said: 'Now to a fashion show. . . .' But these ruins were here, larger than two feet square; they would not go away.

All these things made with care were fit for nothing any more. Machines had made them; hands had made the machines. It wasn't junk or scrap or rubbish simply to be swept out of harm's way; these broken things were the work of human hands, patient years of human time. It was sad to see them here smashed beyond repair, in a second of violence destroyed, made loathsome in an instant by the tragedy they foretold.

Over the edge; somewhere down there.

He leant farther and farther to the side trying to see. It was like a cliff falling into nowhere. Nothing was there except the opalescent cloud.

He couldn't move. The earth held him there. To lift a foot was to raise the planet with it. The planet was too heavy; he couldn't drag it over the edge stuck to the soles of his shoes.

'Somehow I've got to go down, but in the dark I'll fall. I'll get poison all over me. The smell of it's everywhere. Maybe there are acids, chemicals that'll burn. It's too steep to stand. How far down have they gone? Down and down or just a little way?

'Dad. Are you there?'

Why did he call when he knew there could be no reply? Perhaps a spirit would move a tree or touch him like a breeze or lift him bodily from the road and gently let him down.

But he remained drooped, anchored to the ground, toes of his shoes hard up to the ridge of gravel and mud.

'Dad. I've come. Can't you hear?'

But nothing came, not a breeze, not a word.

He was alone and his sadness was as deep as time, as broad as all the people who had ever lived in the world, millions and millions and millions of people all alone.

He fought against everything that held him to the ground. Again and again he felt himself turn, felt his feet lift, felt the wild slide, the slipping and the scramble into a steep place of stones and sticks and cloud, but then looked back with shock and saw himself as before, unmoving, still drooping on the road. It was a sensation so weird that it began to hurt, as though something inside him was forcing its way out of his body then fleeing in dismay back into it. He tried with all the strength he had to stop it and suddenly the wild slide, the slipping and the scramble were real. He was clawing with feet and hands in a shower of pebbles and twigs; rocks were hard, undergrowth was rough, the slope was like a steeple.

He crashed against a tree trunk and it felled him. There was the stink of fungus and decomposing leaves, a deep, wet softness with sharp fragments like thorns that penetrated his clothes. He lay stunned by the force of impact, aching to his teeth.

In a while he groped out of the mould and pulled himself

upright beside the tree and clung to it, spitting dirt from his mouth, rubbing creepy things like spider-webs from his eyes and ears and hair.

Where was the road? Somewhere up in the cloud. For how long had he slid and scrambled? He didn't know; he could draw no line of time between the real event and the others he had imagined. It was an effort of comprehension to accept the tree and the slope and the ankle-deep humus, to accept that everything had suddenly changed, that the mood of sadness up there had gone forever, had belonged to a time that might as well have been years ago. Wreckage lay up there, deadly poisons, solitude, and a half-dream world of imaginings. Up there the window-dressing; down here the things that were real.

He clung to the tree, eyes tightly closed, sweat breaking out of him, hardening his nerve to peer into the fog. He drew strength from the tree, from its roots in the earth, its foliage in the air, its bark against his face.

Two monstrous objects lay on their backs thirty yards apart, one crushed, the other elongated as though pole-axed, stretched out. One was the car. The other was a transport broken in pieces. He saw them as though moonlight was as bright as the sun, then saw nothing but fog.

He held to the tree, blood draining from his head, and looked again but there was nothing but fog.

'I'm the eldest now, in more ways than one.'

Max heard his own voice in a level key and slid down into the leaf-mould in a heap. There were thoughts like a snapshot album. Dad mowing the lawn and cutting the top out of his shoe. Mum with Brenda icing a cake and dropping it in the sink. Dad with Max and Tony painting the house. Mum with David reading a book: 'That's Pooh Bear, that's Christopher Robin, that's Piglet,' and closing the book and weeping for no reason that she would explain. Dad coming home from work. Mum shopping for bright red apples. Dad hearing Tony's spelling and losing his temper bit by bit. Mum holding Max by the hand going to school when he was five. Mum with a bucket of disinfectant cleaning up David's room before he was toilet-trained. Mum and Dad arguing the toss. Mum and Dad smiling. Then there was nothing but fog.

Max dragged himself to his feet and leant against the tree as sometimes he had leant against Dad when he was tired and years younger, then made his way, bent, across the face of the slope, holding on to anything his hands could reach, starting a patter of stones and earth that seemed to have nothing to do with himself. The real things were becoming dream-like again although he tried to keep them clear. There was a sound like wind in his ears, as though he had been propelled head-first into air. There was squeamishness, trembling and an awful shortage of breath. He dug in his heels to prevent the slip and sat heavily beside the car.

'Dad?'

He knew they were dead. He had known all along. He didn't really have to ask.

'Mum?'

He sat there for a long while, turning numb with cold, head on knees, eyes shut, empty except for wind sounds in his ears, sometimes close, sometimes distant, an endlessly sighing wind although not a leaf stirred.

When he looked up he saw through the fog as he had seen through it before, brilliant moonlight flashed on a screen, and the transport lower down was like something that had been lifted by one end and thrown. He didn't want to leave the car; it was his vigil, he would sit there until he froze, he would sit there until he died; but another pull of compelling power urged him to move. He answered it against everything that rebelled against stirring, the inertia in him, the stiffness, the deeply penetrating cold, the dog-like devotion to those few square yards of hillside. He crabbed down the slope in physical pain, in an anguish of loyalty betrayed, and didn't stand until he could reach the trailer with his hands. He dragged himself upright against it, wincing from the cold, enveloped in fog that rolled back silently, and having got there didn't know why he had come.

He leant against the truck as he had leant against the tree, as sometimes he had leant against Dad when he was tired. He groped round in the shadows of his mind trying to fasten on to thoughts that would tell him what to do. Nothing stayed long enough to hold. The deep-down Max seemed to have gone away; all that was left was a chilled body without a working will of its own.

Again that blind compulsion came and he stumbled along the wreckage to the cabin that was upside down. The earth was different, slippery, but not with cyanide. It was oil.

'Are you there?' he said.

Nothing replied.

In a timid way he tapped on the side. 'Are you there?' There was no answering call, but something drew him on, a feeling unlike the certainty of death he had had near the car. The deep-down Max began to stir; a sensation almost of pins and needles rawly awakened his nerves.

'Hey!'

He banged against the side.

'You in there!'

Smell came to him in a wave; not the smell of fuel or of oil, but of sickness.

A voice said, 'Yes, Dad. I'm still here.'

It was a girl.

'I'm not your Dad,' Max said, but suddenly choked on it. They were alive and didn't have anybody like David at home.

'Yes, Dad. What do you want? . . . Dad, are you all right? Why did you call?'

Max burst out with bitterness. 'I'm not your Dad. I'm not your Dad. You've killed my Mum and Dad; that's what you've done.' Then he cried.

The sobs of the boy were different from the strange words that had floated for so long in the silence, the words that had had little to do with time or place and even now seemed like inscriptions read from headstones in cemeteries where pioneers were buried; those sad inscriptions that were so funny and quaint that you had to cry inside even though they were far from the world of everyday. But the sobs were not like that, nor was the boy, they were real and close and belonged to the world of motor cars and chromium-plated steel.

Alison did not interrupt; she let him cry.

There was something sacred about it, demanding respect, that went beyond the hurt of being unjustly accused of killing his Mum and Dad. And there was something right about it that fitted her own situation. It was right that someone should stand beside the wreck and cry.

'Dad,' she said, 'someone's come. Can't you hear?'

The boy cried as though he had saved up his heartbreak for a lifetime before letting go and then became quiet, so quiet that she thought he had gone away.

'Dad,' she said, 'answer me.'

But everything was still for a time that dragged and dragged, and when she tried to ask more questions nothing came. Were even the aches, the bruises and the cold, memories of something different that had happened to her long ago? Was the boy who had cried perhaps part of a radio play she had heard? Then there were sniffing sounds that formed into words. 'Are you hurt?' Were these words, too, from long ago or were they happening now? 'I'm sorry I said you killed my Mum and Dad. I know you couldn't help it. But—it's never happened before.'

Something was wrong with that but exactly what Alison didn't know. She heard it, then it was gone and she couldn't put it together again. 'Don't cry,' she said, knowing it was the wrong thing to say.

'I'm not crying.' It was not a heated denial but a bewildered one. 'I wasn't crying.' But he ended in confusion. Something about his voice was gentle for a boy.

'How did you get out of the car? The crash was such a long time ago.'

'I wasn't in it.' He sounded surprised, as if she should have known. 'It was Mum and Dad coming back from the train. We were all at home. Not exactly home. We come here at holiday time. Brenda and Tony and David and me and Mum and Dad. Seven years we've been coming here. I suppose it's finished now.' He ended in confusion again, and asked (ashamed, because he thought he had forgotten to ask before), 'Are you hurt?'

'I don't know.'

'You must know.'

'I don't, I don't. I don't know.'

'What about your Dad?'

'I don't know about Dad either. He doesn't answer me any more. I'm not sure now that he ever did. I thought I was talking to him, but I don't know. Perhaps he was thrown out, not here at all.'

'What's your name?'

'Alison. What's yours?'

'Maxwell Stirling Shaw.'

'All of it? All the time?'

'Max will do.' But he sounded confused again. 'I'm fifteen,' he said. 'How old are you?'

'Fourteen.'

It was strange.

'I can't reach you,' he said, 'something's in the way. Do you think I'd better break the door? I can see you. I can see your hair. Turn your head around. Your hair's fair like Brenda's. Have you got freckles, too?'

'I can't turn my head around,' she said, 'not all the way round there. I'm lying on my side.'

'I wish you could,' he said.

'I can't.'

'Please.'

'I can't, I can't. Really I can't.'

'You're not hurt?'

'I don't know.'

'Gee, you mustn't be hurt, Alison. That'd be awful. Are you cold? Could you put my coat over you if I push it through?'

'I can't move my hands. I'm jammed in. Anyway, you need it more than I do. You're outside.'

'You're not hurt, Alison?'

'No,' she said.

'Gee, that's great. Gee, you're lucky. You just can't imagine what it looks like from the outside.'

She could hear him hammering at the door, perhaps with a stone, and heaving at it for a while. Then she knew he was picking out remnants of glass a piece at a time. 'You're real fair,' he said, 'like Brenda. Have you got freckles, too?'

'A few.'

Suddenly, something touched her hair, a hand, and suddenly drew away.

'You're real. It's you that I can see.' His voice was eager but strained. It made her feel warm and for a moment or two her cheeks burned. Then he said, 'What was your father doing, bringing a transport way out here?'

'He was lost and couldn't turn round.'

'He could have turned if he'd gone up to the Lookout. Bags of room there.'

'But he didn't.'

'Too bad.'

'Will you see if you can reach my Dad?'

'You're upside down.'

'But will you try?'

'Is your name McPhee?'

'Yes.'

'It's on the door. Did you come from Scotland or were you born here?'

'Here.'

The position of his voice changed. She tried to imagine what he was like, but couldn't somehow. What he looked like was *very* important.

'You're dark,' she said, 'aren't you?'

'Yes, very dark at times. It's the fog. It seems to come and go.'

'Not the fog. You!'

'I suppose so.' The voice seemed to come from far away.

'Don't leave me,' she said.

'I'm here.'

'Are you tall or short?'

'I'm tall and thin. What about you?'

She didn't answer.

'What about you, Alison?'

'I don't know. Nothing special. Average, I suppose.' Then she said, 'Are you six feet?'

'Five feet eleven. Dad reckons I'll go to six-two. But I won't be thin then, you'll see.' His voice changed again; it came through loud and clear as though in a closed room. 'Alison . . .'

'I heard,' she said. 'Six-two. That's tall.'

'I'm not talking about tall. I mean your Dad. He's here. Are there only the two of you?'.

'Yes,' she said, 'I haven't got a mother any more.'

He sounded puzzled. 'No . . . In the cab. Here.'

'Yes. Only two. Anybody there has got to be Dad.'

She heard a grunt, but no words.

'Max?'

She heard his breathing, but still no words.

'Tell me, Max.'

'I'm awfully sorry, Alison. He's cold.'

'You mean he's dead?'

'I reckon so. For quite a while.'

She felt empty; felt nothing at all. Oh, it was awful that she could feel nothing at all when any decent girl would have wept and wailed. What sort of a person would Max think she was? Max had cried and cried and he was a boy who'd grow to six feet two, but she couldn't feel anything, couldn't even see her Dad in her mind, could remember only vague things like smoke-filled cafés at two o'clock in the morning (Dad turning his head away to talk to a man), and a straight back at the wheel (face not seen), and trunk-line telephone calls from far-away places in the evening at school (Dad not there in flesh and blood, only his voice in a moulded plastic case held to her ear).

'Dad's eyes were blue,' she said. 'He was five-eleven, too. The kids reckoned he was a smasher. The Sixth Formers said they could go for him in a big way. They didn't know he was a truckie. Maybe they'd have changed their minds if they'd known.' But by then she was crying, somehow glad and torn through with pain at the same time.

She scarcely knew that Max's hand had returned to her side of the cab and was laid gently on her hair.

ELEVEN

State of Mind

BRENDA DRAGGED HER feet, stricken with the cold of the water from the spring. She had plunged in her hands, there was no slime on them now, but she was numbed to the marrow of her bones, the chill of the water aching deeper and deeper even after she left the spring behind. Was the chill more deadly than the poison washed off?

The hillside going down was a haze in which she had lost her way, in which every dragging step was the same as the one before. The night fenced her about with walls of cold that she could not pass through, the walls moved with her like a cage. Only her thoughts ran free, breaking out of the cage, and their freedom was a wildness she could not control. She knew they were stupid, that her mind took her to places where she'd rather not go, that her thoughts should have been held very firmly down. As Dad often said: 'For a practical young lady you can panic like a fool.'

But it was cold, it was cold, and down below in the shack beside the lake Tony half-asleep was waiting on her word. What could she say to Tony? He adored his Dad. What could she say to David? How would David ever be made to understand?

'They're dead, David. They've gone away. God's taken them to Heaven. Heaven's in the sky. I don't know where Heaven is. Oh golly, what can I say? I'm sorry, David, I wouldn't have had it happen to you for worlds. I can't bring them back, David. There's nothing I can do. It's the end. Like a story that comes to the end and it's gone. It's not like the wolf in the fairy-tale. You can't cut it open and get the people back again. But do you know what I mean when I talk about a story? Do you know what a story is?

'Tony, you try. You tell David. Sometimes you can get through to him. But first Tony himself has got to understand. Oh, David, what will we do with you? Put you in a home? People were always at Mum to put you in a home. People always said to her that carting you miles every day to the Training Centre was mad, that she was wearing herself into the ground.

'You're nothing now, David. You're nobody any more. Just a dim-witted little kid that nobody will bother with, that nobody will understand. I can't look after you, David; I don't know how. I've got to go to school. I'm not fifteen till January 23rd next year. I'll never be a teacher if I leave school now. All of us are nobodies now. That's what Gran always says; a woman's nothing without a man. Well, what are kids without a Mum and Dad? No one to earn the wages or cook the meals. They won't let kids stay in a house on their own. There's only Gran and she lives miles away and Dad always reckons she's too old to raise an arm. There's only Auntie Pru and she's got five kids of her own. There's only Uncle Bert and we haven't seen him in years. There's only Aunt Monica and she's a teacher in New Guinea. Maybe they'll put all of us in an orphanage. What else can they do?'

She came into the carport under the shack, not remembering how she had got there, for the moment not believing that she had. She had broken out of the cage with the walls of cold. To stumble into the carport was not to arrive, but to escape from something bad. But why had she come? 'Go home,' Max had said, 'and get back as quickly as you can.' It was the cyanide, not only on her hands, but on her clothes.

She kicked off her shoes, shuddering with emotion to be rid of them, and pulled off her coat and her jeans hating the touch of them, and with surprise found her nightdress underneath. Then remembered putting it on to go to bed years and years ago; the world had turned over since then, turned over out of the light and gone cold.

Suddenly, she was aware of the gaping space where the car should have been.

There was only a glimmer left in Tony's little torch, but enough to register the emptiness that was there and to make it real enough for her to flinch inside. The car would never come now or it would have overtaken her on the road, or if Dad had been stopped by the obstructions at the bend he would have sounded the horn. Max would have caught him at the bend and told him what to do. The horn would have blasted on the hill to let Brenda know. The sounding of the horn would have been something to remember for the rest of her life with joy. Why couldn't the horn have made that sound?

She could feel the emptiness all around and had never realized before how warm it was when the car was there.

The car meant things like Mum upstairs, like going back to school again in a day or two, like Christmas coming at the end of next term, like weekdays and weekends full of ordinary things, such as driving to piano lessons on Wednesday at five. All the ordinary things that were gone, that were changed.

It was cold; it was so cold.

Oh, that empty space where the car should have been was more terrifying by its silence than the accident with all its noise. Imagine kicking off her clothes like this to leave them here, never to be driven over, or crushed by wheels, or dripped on by oil. How suddenly the habits of a lifetime changed. She could undress in the carport and leave her clothes lying here. She could leave clothes anywhere, in heaps on floors, in piles on chairs. Wear them dirty, if she wanted to, there was no one to care. Slam the doors if she wanted to; go barefoot round the house; fill the bath to the brim if she wanted to, never be nagged because water slopped under the door into the hall. She could fry bacon and onions every afternoon after school, watch adult shows on TV, cut her hair short like a boy's, give Bible Class the skip and lie in bed on Sundays until half-past ten. All these things she had wanted to do. She would give the lot for one shrill call: 'Brenda, will you get out of that bath and give someone else a go.' 'Brenda, will you make your bed.' 'Brenda, the dirty dishes have been waiting for an hour.' 'Brenda, why must I shout? Why can't you do things when you're told?' Mum's call, like the car, would not come again. There was no one to disobey, so why bother to disobey any more?

Upstairs Tony was waiting on her word.

She climbed the ramp to the door, as though it were a mountain. What was she to say? What would Tony do? Would David understand or laugh in his usual way?

The door gave to her hand and opened with a scraping sound, opened half-way and grated on the floor.

'Tony,' she said timidly, 'are you there?' Then heard herself after she had spoken the words and despised herself for the wishy-washy tone. Something positive in her momentarily stirred. 'Tony! You didn't shut the door. You know better than that by now. You know you're not to leave it ajar.'

A pulse of emptiness came back to her, almost as if the emptiness down below where the car should have been had come up through the floor.

'Tony! It's me. It's Brenda. Are you there?'

In the torchlight she saw the broken lock and wood splintered at the side. She felt strangely disturbed and handled the lock uneasily and said aloud, 'What would he break it for? Hey, Tony, what did you break the lock for? Hey, David, what about you?'

No one was there.

She went first to David's room, then to Tony's, and lapsed again into confusion and couldn't think coherently. Questions were everywhere. Was there a note? She hunted for one in a half-hearted way then forgot what she was trying to do. Had the boys followed in the fog when Max had gone with her up to the bend? If they had, wouldn't she have met them on the road?

'Hey, Tony,' she said, 'where have you gone? Why did you break the lock?' Or had she said that before?

It was awfully cold.

'Our first female Prime Minister in the making,' Dad used to say, long ago, before this night began. Perhaps, if he could see her now, he wouldn't use the same words.

She reached for the nearest light switch on the wall, questioning herself for allowing the torch to waste away, but the pale glimmer from the ceiling reminded her that the lighting plant needed recharging. She thought then of the candle left burning when she had gone out with Max and saw the flame in her mind, as though separated from her by years and miles. It was an effort to move herself across to the kitchen side. Nothing remained of the candle except a congealed puddle of wax. It was a greater effort still to open a cupboard and get out another candle. She stood with it in her hand for a minute or two before the next impulse came, then she struck a match and laboriously set the candle in the holder.

It was early morning on a winter's day and there were things to do. Mechanically, she filled the kettle and placed it over a low gas flame, and took the candle with her to the bathroom. There, as usual, she turned on the shower and held out her hands until the water ran hot; terribly hot this morning; it seared her like fire and she cried out in pain. She recoiled in surprise against the shower-recess wall and frantically fiddled with taps to cool it down, but its heat drew her in again, hurting excruciatingly, but healing her at the same time. Heat poured over her, dissolving the cold, beating at her until she glowed. It was as beautiful as midsummer's sun and she didn't want to leave it, wanted only to stand there in clouds of steam and melt. If it had not been for a puzzling stab of conscience—Max waiting on the hillside—she might have stayed until the water turned cold. She had come to the shack only to change her clothes!

Roughly, she towelled herself down and hurried with the candle to her bedroom, there to scramble into the warmest clothes and the stoutest shoes she could quickly find, yet then to stand motionless again, appalled. What of Tony?

What of David? What of the broken lock on the door? Or
were they imagined things like the state of mind that must
have put her under the shower?

'Tony! David! Are you there?'

Of course they were not there. Of course they were gone.
And there was a kettle whistling lazily on the stove. What
time was it? Nearly half-past four! Where were the boys?
Why weren't Tony and David at home? It was awfully
foolish of Tony to venture outside. There must have been
more to this than met the eye. It really was stupid of Tony
to go away. Oh golly, oh golly, what did it mean? She
could feel the weight and the pressures of her worries
building up again, but there was an equal determination
not to sink back into despair. She went with busy steps to the
stove, busily found a cup, opened the coffee jar, and with
purpose drank it black and as hot as she could stand,
fighting off the threat of the anxieties that lay beyond the
outside door. Out there were things that she feared as she
had feared nothing at any other time. The yearning to run
to her room, to bury her face in the pillow, to surrender to
her grief, to have nothing more to do with anything, was
almost too much to bear, but she drank her coffee black
and scalding hot and held on grimly to her nerve.

What was next? Where did she go from here? Did she
really want to know? No! Things were enough as they were
without knowing in advance the events of the next hour or
the next year.

She blew out the candle and went back to the outside door.
Was the fog less dense? It might have been. There was a
suspicion of moonlight shining on water, a lengthening
moonbeam, a moon sinking towards the mountain ridges on
the far side of the dam.

She couldn't go out; she couldn't.

It was so silent out there except for creaking sounds, trees
groaning in the cold. The sense of aloneness cut her off
from all the things she knew how to do best. She liked to be
boss of a crowd, to be captain of the team, to excel. ('That's
Brenda Shaw; she goaled *fourteen* times against Camberwell
High.' 'Brenda got her First Class Badge when she was only

thirteen.' 'Brenda knows the words. She knows them all. Sing it for us, Brenda.') When kids were around Brenda was Queen. All that seemed a hundred years ago.

She turned the torch-beam on her eyes. She'd be lucky if it lasted another quarter-hour, but she'd have to go, because she was the mother now. Something about the thought appealed to her, but the broken lock was like a nagging voice at her side. Why was it there? An impatience flared in her, a feeling of resentment that turned into a screech, 'Tony! Come back here. What do you mean by going away? You naughty boy.'

Her throat suddenly hurt and her ears rang. A beautiful world that had usually been kind seemed to have gone completely mad. She sat on the step and nursed her face in her hands.

'You're the mother now. You've got to go.'

'I'm only fourteen.'

'You've got to go.'

'I can't go. I don't know where to go. I can't go back up the hill until I know what has happened to the boys.'

There was a sound she had not noticed before; a purr; it might almost have been inside her. In an instant she found herself on the road with no memory of having moved from the door.

There were headlights in the fog. Were they uphill or down? In her confusion she didn't know. She ran towards them, afraid they would disappear, but in a moment that she would never understand suddenly wished that they were not there. She heard Tony shout, 'Brenda, Brenda. Did you find Mum and Dad?'

A lamp flashed in her eyes and a strange voice said, 'Has he come home? Have you got the little boy?' It was a man. The light turned off to one side.

A woman said, 'Brenda, my dear.'

The doors of the car opened and Tony tumbled out to pull on Brenda's arm. 'David's come back, hasn't he? David's come home. What about Mum and Dad?'

The man emerged curiously, like a fade-in on a screen. 'Quietly, Tony. Brenda, David's run away.'

The woman said again (Brenda couldn't see her), 'Brenda, my dear.'

'You didn't find Mum and Dad, did you? Oh, Mr Fenwick, she didn't find Mum and Dad. Oh, Brenda, David's run away; he ran out the door. We've been everywhere. I can't find Fatso; I've called and called and called. Oh, Brenda, we don't know which way he's gone.'

'All right, lad,' the man said, 'that's enough now. We'll know in time. We'll find him soon. I want to hear what Brenda has to say.'

She couldn't frame a word.

'Has there been an accident, Brenda?'

She nodded.

'Your mother and father?'

She burst out. 'I don't know. There's cyanide up there. Drums and drums of it. Everywhere.'

'But not your mother and father?'

'I don't know. But I know just the same. I've known all the time.'

The woman said, 'Cyanide can't have anything to do with your parents, Brenda. And how do you know it's cyanide anyway?'

'Because it's written on the drums. I saw, I saw. I had to come back to wash it off myself, to change my clothes. Max is still up there, all on his own.'

'It doesn't sound like your parents to me,' the woman said in an unvarying tone, 'it sounds like a truck that's overturned. Your parents are miles away, child, with a blowout or a breakdown or waiting for the fog to clear.'

'They're not,' Brenda said, 'I know, I know. They wouldn't do this to us. They'd have got home somehow. They're so fussy about these things. If they weren't so fussy it wouldn't have happened at all. I know, I know. I'll bet they were driving like mad. I'll bet Dad was growling at Mum all the way for leaving us behind. She'd never done it before.' The identity of the people she was speaking to occurred to her almost by surprise. 'Mr Fenwick, I *know*.'

Tony held her hand and Brenda could see both of the

Fenwicks now; the man with an arm thrust rigidly over the door of his car, the woman half-seated in the back with one leg to the ground. The only movement, just then, came from the car. The engine idled, steam from the exhaust drifted red through the tail-light glow, the windscreen wipers clicked back and forth, headlamps created a luminous haze. The click of the wipers was like a slow clock stretching time.

The woman said, 'Frank; what will you do?'

'It's a question of priorities,' he said.

'I know.'

'Lord,' he said, 'what will we do?'

'You can't stand here.'

'I know.'

'Frank; make up your mind.'

'People might be dying up there. A lost child down here. Cyanide up there. You ask me to make up my mind? These drums, Brenda; are they broken?'

'Lots of them are. They're in the ditch and on the road. Like marbles. And there's red stuff; awful red stuff, too. Golly, Mr Fenwick, what'll we do? What if David's gone that way? He can't read. He won't understand.'

'What does he usually do when he runs away?'

'We never *let* him run away. There are snibs on all the doors, bolts on all the gates. At home we've fences seven feet high. Someone watches him all the time. How did he ever get out, Tony? He should never have got away.'

The man said, 'Listen, Brenda. He's out. It's my fault. He's out. But you can't tell me he has *never* got away. Think, think. What does he do when he runs away?'

'He hides,' Tony said. 'He *hides*. And doesn't make a sound. Then he laughs and you find him when he laughs.'

'Sometimes he hides in a cupboard,' Brenda said, 'or in the woodshed or under the house. But when he gets out of the gate he runs. He goes nowhere special, except that he turns to the right. Never the other way. Runs and runs until he's tired. Then he lies down.'

'How do you know that? Always to the right?'

Brenda was suddenly confused. 'I don't know,' she said.

'I've never thought of it before, but it's true. We always find him up Luke Street way at home, never down the other way.'

'What happens when he gets away here?'

'He never has.'

'He must have done.'

'Never, never. We take such special care, because of the lake. Or else he never tries. I don't know.'

'You mean you watch him *all* the time?'

'We've got to, unless we put him in his room and lock the door.'

The man turned to his wife but she drew her leg deliberately back into the car and said in a dreary monotone, 'Come on, Frank. Decide, decide. You're wasting time.'

'How can I decide? It's life and death whichever way I go and the facts are not clear. Am I God to decide whose life comes first? It's too much for one man.'

There seemed to be a sigh. 'There are no other men, Frank Fenwick, so it's got to be you.'

'You're not helping by pressuring me. Let me think.'

'You've had hours to think. It took me thirty minutes to get you to move.'

'For heaven's sake, Phyllis; not here, please.'

'Your contributions so far,' she said in the same grey voice, 'are the melodrama of a broken door and a simpleminded creature running loose.'

'And you've never made a mistake in your life, I suppose?'

'You should have found him then and there, Frank, before he had a chance to go bush, then your "mistake", as you call it, would have mattered less.'

'You were not here, Phyllis. You don't understand. The lad and I, we tried. We must have searched forty minutes or more.'

She made a clicking sound with her tongue and Brenda felt Tony's tightening hand and in herself bewilderment and dismay. Dad had always said they were not his kind of people.

'There was no script, Phyllis,' the man said, clipping each word, 'it wasn't on camera, you know. The next movement was not written down as it is for you. We had to play it by ear.'

'It's a pity you didn't. If you had listened you would have heard the child. He couldn't run away without making a noise. And you heard what the girl said. He's probably under the house or in a cupboard or locked in the lavatory.'

The man's hand went to his brow.

'Then you had to come home like a little boy to me,' she said remorselessly.

'For another pair of legs,' he said angrily, 'for another pair of eyes. I'm sorry if I had to get you out of bed.'

'And while you're away he could fall in the dam with no one to hear his scream. There are times, Frank, when I despair for you.' She leant suddenly across the car seat and pressed heavily on the horn (a cruel and unexpected sound) then called sternly with studied diction into the night; 'David Shaw. We are on the road near your house. Come at once, boy, come along. Then the cause of Fenwick's indecision will be removed.'

Tony tugged persistently on Brenda's hand, communicating plainly without words, and Brenda's dismay turned into something like calm, 'If you'll excuse us, Mr Fenwick,' she said, 'I think we'll go.'

'What?' the woman said. 'Go where?'

Brenda felt towards her almost nothing at all, only dislike and a need made certain by the demanding pressure of Tony's hand to get away from her as soon as she could. But Mum wouldn't like her to be rude.

'We'd rather be on our own,' Brenda said, 'thank you all the same. You've been very kind.'

Then Tony ran, dragging on her hand, dragging her after him, stammering almost with tears, 'She's a witch, she's a witch, I know she's a witch. I'll spit in her eye.'

They ran out of the glow into the grey.

'Brenda! Tony!' It was the man calling from behind. 'Come back here.'

Tony wailed, 'She wouldn't believe what he said . . .'

'Afterwards, afterwards. Let's get away.'

'She called him names.'

'Afterwards, Tony.'

They heard the car doors slam and they scrambled from the road into the bush at the side.

'Lie still,' panted Brenda. 'Keep low. Wait till they've gone.'

'Sis, what are we going to do?'

'Look for David. He won't have got far.'

'But he went ages ago.'

'Be quiet. They'll hear.'

The car went past in a sphere of light and the man called again, almost plaintively, 'Come back, kids. Everything's all right now.'

'He's a nice man.'

'Shhh.' Then Brenda hissed, 'If I see her again *I'll* spit in her eye.'

'Too right,' said Tony, 'we'll both spit in her eye.'

'Come on,' said Brenda, 'we'll go up through the bush. I'll bet David's gone that way. Don't let go of my hand.'

'She's a horrible woman, and she's so nice on TV.'

'I suppose you tried the shacks?'

'Of course we did. All the way from Harley's to Fenwick's.'

Some distance off they heard the man call, 'Answer me, kids. You haven't got a chance on your own.'

TWELVE

Like Heaven was a Hand

ALISON BECAME AWARE of a soothing source of warmth against her head. It was like a knitted cap made especially for her, yet unmistakably a hand. Scarcely ever had anyone placed a hand on her head; occasionally a teacher passing by her desk; never Dad. It was not one of his ways. Suddenly, she wished it had been—or would a commonplace act have spoiled the moment now? This tender awareness of a boy, of someone she seemed to have known all her life. He had always been there—out of sight, even as he was still—waiting for the moment to place his hand upon her head.

All at once she had nothing to cry about any more. She was glad the tears had come because it would not have been right for Dad to have gone away without them, but she was glad they were over. It was true; Dad was not the sort of man you could wail for. Wailing over Dad seemed as wrong as no tears at all. Dad was more like a noisy chorus of merry-making men singing out of tune than a heartbroken dirge. Dad had gone. Max had come.

She wished more and more that she could see him; she wished she could free an arm to reach up for his hand. In a way that hand was the same as a telephone to her ear. There was a great distance between them.

'Max,' she said, not asking a question, not expecting a reply.

'Alison.' He knew what she meant because he said

nothing other than her name and that was enough for a while.

'Max, I love your hand there but you'd better take it away. I'm dirty. I've been sick.'

'I don't care. I don't mind.'

It didn't seem strange in the least to be huddled against the wreck with one aching arm extended inside. Elsewhere he was acutely cold and miserably wet and vaguely aware of terrible things, but where his hand touched her head a tiny fire glowed with a cosy flame. He had never felt a bond like this with any person before. The fire in his hand seemed to be the reason for the world, for a thousand things worth thinking of that until now had never crossed his mind, that didn't belong to the boy his family knew. It was as beautiful as being alone, as not having to strike a pose, but it was more than that; there was nothing troublesome about it, nothing that bothered him, only a wonderful calm strangely related to sadness, yet different in an unfathomable way.

'You'll ring me at school, Max.'

Of course he would. 'Yes, Alison.'

'Any time between 6.30 and 8.00. Dad doesn't ring every night. Sometimes he can't.'

He thought about that. Poor Alison. Part of her acknowledged that her father was dead, but the rest of her didn't know. It must be awful to lose a father when there wasn't a mother at home. He remembered her saying something about her mother but it was ages ago, before she had cried.

'When did your mother die?'

'She didn't. She went away when I was four. I don't know why, except that Dad said she was cold. About being a mother, I think. He said keep the bath hot. Wasn't that a funny thing to say? Do you think I imagined it all? That he was dead all the time?'

The question drifted away from Max or didn't get through.

'Your mother left home. That's strange. Mine won't leave the house at all, hardly. The way she went on about it tonight—' And that thought, too, drifted away. 'Mondays and Thursdays I won't be able to ring you. Other nights are all right. Mondays I learn the guitar, Thursdays I go to

Scouts. Sometimes at weekends we're not home; we come up here. Why are you at school at that time of day?'

'Boarding school.' She was surprised that he hadn't known. 'I've been there since I was six.'

'Do you like it?'

'Why not?'

'What school is it?'

'St Clare's.'

After a while he whistled.

'What did you do that for?'

'It's a classy sort of school. Gee, I didn't know you went to St Clare's.' Somehow, he wished he hadn't put it quite that way, but the words were said, they were gone, and he felt a subtle change in the emotion flowing back to him through his hand.

'Why shouldn't I go to St Clare's?' she said. 'Because my Dad's a truckie?'

'No, no, no.' He felt awful because she had caught him out on an attitude that wasn't right and both of them knew that his denial was a lie. He couldn't allow the lie to stay. 'I suppose I did mean it,' he said. 'I'm sorry. I suppose I was surprised.' He felt wretched and cold; even his hand was going cold; but her head moved to press more firmly against his touch and the panic went away.

'Max; do you like playing the guitar?'

'Yeh. Yeh, I do. I've been learning for three years.'

'Do you sing, too?'

'Only a bit. Brenda's the one with the voice. She knows lots of folk songs. I forget the words. Tony sings all right. Boy soprano. He's a wild one, too, when he wants to be, but when he sings he's like a bell, and his face is like an angel's. The rest of the time his face is like the back of a bus. Funny, isn't it!'

'Brenda's your sister?'

'Yeh. Didn't I say? A real bossy-britches. She's a bit of a pain. She's captain of everything. Are you captain of anything at school?'

'No.'

'Are you top of the form?'

'Me? Not me.'

'I'm glad.'

'Are you?'

'Yeh. I hate girls who are too clever or too bossy.'

After a pause, she said, 'Someone's got to be top.'

'Yeh. But I don't want it to be you.'

'Because you want to be cleverer than me?'

'No. Not that.'

'What then?'

'Don't really know. Do I have to?'

She felt a flutter of alarm. 'Of course not.' It was becoming harder to keep everything on an even keel. Face to face there wouldn't be these differences; it was so awfully like talking on the telephone. 'Let's say nothing for a while.'

'All right.' His arm was aching terribly, but he didn't mind. Then he started thinking about her in another way, trying to picture her, conjuring up faces that might fit her voice, but every face he imagined was the face of someone else he knew, of girls at school, of girls he had seen in the street, and of one particular girl seen only for an hour in a train. Something in him had reached out to that girl, a little like this but not the same. 'I bet your Dad has to work hard to send you to St Clare's.'

'Sometimes,' she said, 'but not always. He's an odd bod, is Dad. Sometimes he works like mad. Other times I think he goes on a binge and spends half of what he earns.'

Something about that seemed sad. Max couldn't imagine such a father fitting in with a girl like Alison. 'You don't mean he gets drunk, do you?'

'Yes, I do. He's a bit of a lad is Dad. It's when he doesn't ring me at school. When he misses two or three nights. Other times he rings me up from Sydney, even. More than three dollars for the call.'

'I don't think I've ever seen my Dad drunk. I don't know that he ever has been. Unless it was during the war, before I was born.'

Nothing happened then, for almost a minute. Max's brain emptied out, appalled, until Alison cut in, 'I don't suppose it matters now. It never used to worry me much.

You get used to your Dad. It's only tonight, thinking about things. He gets silly and shows off.'

Max struggled to hold on to the emptiness in his brain, fearing the angry thought that was demanding expression, and the hot spot where his hand rested on her head began to nag at him again, began to feel like something unclean, that should not have happened at all. Several times the question welled up, several times he forced it back, then it was out— like an explosion in a quiet room. 'Was he drunk tonight?'

He heard the intake of her breath, then a sigh that seemed like the surface escape of a very deep hurt, but she didn't sound heated or outraged, only slow and puzzled. 'Of course not . . .' Her apparent perplexity was real. How could *Max* say a thing like that?

'But you said—'

'I didn't mean it that way.' Sudden anxieties began to break through. 'Not *that*, Max. If that's what it sounded like it's not what I meant. Dad wouldn't drink on the job.' Even to express the thought was disloyal. 'No pep pills or anything like that, either. Dad's strong.' She saw him at the wheel with a straight back. 'It's only when he lets go, Max, and he never lets go on the job. He only lets go when he's tired or fed up. You must know what I mean. *No, Max, no.*'

But he wasn't sure and for the moment he was afraid to put his doubt into words again, and said nothing. To Alison his silence was a dreadful happening. 'On my life, Max,' she shrilled. 'I swear it.'

'Then what was he doing right out here?' As he said it his hand was beginning to draw away, and a hardness, a harshness, a bitterness splintered behind his eyes.

Alison felt his fingers go; the nerves of her scalp felt naked and exposed. 'I told you, I told you. He was lost. Looking for somewhere to turn.'

'A truck driver? Lost? An interstate driver? Lost!'

'Max, Max, why are you saying these things? Yes, he was lost.'

But Max had drawn his aching arm out all the way and it had fallen at his side. He groaned with the change of position, with the pain, with pins-and-needles running wild.

'No truckie would ever come this way. What would he come out here for? In the middle of the night? In a fog? Never, unless he was half-sprung. You're trying to cover up for him.' The pain in his arm was almost more than he could bear. It felt as though it was falling off. And there were other feelings, bewilderment and disappointment.

She cried, 'No, Max, no. I'm not covering up. It's true. It was *because* of the fog. He knows a man in a pub, Fred Finn—'

'Yeh, yeh. In a pub!'

'Fred said to call on him any night and stay. Not tonight. He didn't say it tonight. He said it other times. Weeks ago. Months ago. I don't know when. I don't even know this Fred man.'

'I'll bet no one else does, either.'

'Fred said he lived on this road, twenty-three miles from Hamer. That's why Dad came, because of the fog, because he didn't want to go on. I was asleep. I didn't even know. But he couldn't find the place. He couldn't find it. It wasn't there.'

'Anyone could have told you that. There's no one out here called Finn.'

'We know that now, but we didn't know it then. We found out. Max, I'm not making it up. Dad said Fred was probably spinning a yarn. Dad said why this road of all the roads he had to pick to spin a yarn about. I heard him say it *after* the accident. That's when I heard it, *after* the accident—so he must have been alive for a while. Don't you see? Then this car went past coming from the other way and Dad said he would go on and turn, that it was too cold to sit all night on the road. Dad wouldn't drive when he was drunk. He never drinks when I'm around. I've only seen him drunk when I've caught him by surprise. The kids at school reckon he's a smasher. He is, too.' Then the judgement turned in on herself and she couldn't hear Max even though he was trying to make himself heard. 'What did I ever say it for? What did I ever think it for? Max, you've got to believe me. Would I tell a lie to you? Max, put your hand back on my head. It'll be all right then, I know. Oh, Max, I don't know why I said he got drunk. It was a silly thing to say. It's got nothing to do with you at all. All sorts of terrible things I've thought about my Dad tonight, but not one of them was fair. I was only saying what I'd been thinking, and I thought it all *before* the accident, hours ago. I'd take it all back if I could. I'd unthink it all if I could. But I've done it now. Put your hand back, Max. On my life, I swear it, I swear it, I'm not telling a lie.'

His brain was reeling and he believed her as he had believed nothing in his life, but he couldn't make himself heard.

'I believe you, Alison,' he wailed. 'I do, I do. It's got nothing to do with my hand. I can't lift up my arm. It's got nothing to do with what you said. I'm trying, Alison, but I've got pins-and-needles in my arm. It's hurting like mad. Pins-and-needles Alison. I can't lift up my arm.'

Suddenly, she heard. 'I know you don't believe me, I know, I know. It's only an excuse, your arm. I suppose you'll go away and I'll never even see you. You'll go away and you'll forget you ever knew me. The girls all say that boys go away, that boys don't care. It's not your arm, it's not your arm.'

His wail became a moan. 'It's *not* an excuse and I *won't* go away. Oh, gee . . . You're worse than Brenda with a bee in her bonnet. Honest injun, Alison, *listen* to me.' Then his arm answered the frantic urgings of his brain and numbly groped into the wreck and found her again. Peace came down like a miracle, but he was exhausted in a way that he had never been exhausted before. The peace was in Alison like warm breezes, like Heaven was a hand, but not in Max. He felt as though he had run a mile flat out. Golly, oh golly; he had opened a door and a tiger had rushed out and part of him still recoiled in horror, part of him still fled away. It was not like Brenda; it was not like coping with a sister at all. It was like fighting fire. It was like holding back a breach in a dam. He panted beside the wreck shaking from nerves, from cold, and from physical strain, overwhelmed by forces he couldn't understand.

It became quiet again, quieter and quieter, and all the

torments inside ùnravelled like knots falling from a cord. His breathing slowed down, his trembling eased into the ground, a warm spot began to grow again in his hand, and through the hand an emotion flowed as before, the emotion that was related to sadness; as if sadness had two faces and this was the other side; as if the music of sadness that filled the whole world, waiting to be heard, possessed two sounds, one for feeling intensely alone, the other for being with someone in tune with yourself. He was astonished that the feeling came again, the enveloping calm and the tenderness that he could not describe even when its intensity began to embarrass him. A small voice inside him wandered into his consciousness and out again. 'Dad. What is it? Tell me.' But then it didn't matter.

'Max.'

'Yes.'

'You do believe, don't you?'

'You know I do.'

It was all he had needed to say in the first place, but then he had not known the words.

THIRTEEN

The Shivering Places

ONCE A TIME ago (long time? middle time? little time? who could say?) David ran out through a door in the middle of the dark to get away from a light that made the sounds of a man with a big voice. David loved big sounds. They roused in him leapings of delight: big thuds, big bangs, big fallings-over, big breakings, big jumpings, big backfires from motor cars, big smashings, big slammings of doors, big scrapings of beds pushed across hard floors, big dancings of boys and girls throwing each other around, big music turned up loud. But he did not like the light with the big voice of a man, nor Tony's crying, nor the feeling that came through the wall.

It was the feeling he got that made him move his eyes from side to side, made his mouth turn down, made him breathe faster, made him want to run away to somewhere where the trouble wasn't. It was like that but more.

It was like losing the flower the clown gave him; like not eating for many days until he was frail from hunger and his voice went away and no one understood that a pin was in his throat half-way down until he sicked it up in Mummy's hand.

Once another time ago when Mummy smacked hard he climbed through a window pushing a hole in the fly-wire screen in the middle of the dark and wandered through street lights and car lights and the sounds of squealing tyres.

Tyres squealing with delight for a game. Happy night, happy night. Many funny things not to be forgotten. He laughed and laughed and Daddy came all puffing and blowing and shouldering through people and stammering and carried him home on his shoulders. He held to Daddy's hair and pressed his knees into Daddy's neck and Daddy jogged up and down saying, 'David, David, David.'

But Daddy didn't come now and the dark was not like any other dark he knew, not like the dark, lovely and warm, seen from the car, or through the parted curtains of his room when the moon was high, or in the snuggly cupboard under Gran's stairs, or down his wide-open mouth in the mirror. This dark was a long time, like waiting for breakfast after kicking on the wall, or walking with Tony for much too far, holding on to Tony's hand, but so, so tired.

It was a wet dark full of scratchings and pokings and bumps and falls that made him cry. It was a cold dark that made him cough and hurt his feet and dripped from his nose and made his eyelashes all funny; without street lights or car lights or warm lights in windows, without people talking or dogs sniffing at his heels or Jiminy Crickets singing songs in the ground or footsteps clunking on concrete paths. It was a big dark with trunks of trees all the same like people in a crowd who didn't care and rolling stones and steep ups and downs and shivering places and the dam.

He didn't like the dam except to poke his tongue at in broad light of day. It lay there then, all glassy and glazed and a little bit sneery like one of the boys Tony brought home for games. One way the dam called to him, 'Come here.' Another way it growled at him, 'Go away.'

The dam was soft, not nice soft but nasty soft, and toys that fell in didn't come out again. Mummy never understood that he didn't like the dam; it was not like the wading pool on the back lawn a long time away. He would sit in the wading pool until he turned blue with cold and Mummy had to rub him hard with a rough towel and drag him indoors while he dug in his toes. And afterwards he would run outside dodging hands and doors and jump in again in his clothes. Laughing.

David went away from the dam, fearing it as he feared the boy Tony brought home for games. He went up the hill, not down; and across the hill, never down. When there were gullies he wouldn't cross and when big rocks were in the way he went round the uphill side. And when he stopped he remained in one place, remembering hard not to slip down.

As time went by he cried more and more because the dark wouldn't go away and the ache in his ear hurt deeper and deeper and he forgot why he was there.

Was he going to see Gran or Mummy or the clown? Why was Tony not holding his hand? Why was Daddy not riding him on his shoulders jogging up and down? Why was he in the dark not sitting in the car? But the car went away and didn't hear him when he called, went away through the cloud, didn't stop when he called, didn't turn round and come back when he cried.

Why was he cold, so sore cold, so raw cold, so sleepy tired without a bed? Tony should have cuddled up close and talked like a clock.

It was wet where he lay but smelling sweetly with a heavy perfume in the way of certain flowers brought into the house that should have been left outside, certain flowers that were pretty in the garden but too sickly sweet for indoors.

'No, David, you must leave the jonquils outside.'

'No, David, not the lilies. We can't have *them* in the house.'

Even roses, some of them that Daddy grew, had a perfume as heavy as rain pressing down before it tumbled from the sky. Perfume was strange. You couldn't see it or hold it but you could feel it like a wind or a feather. You could look for it everywhere but never find it. All you could find were the things it came from and sometimes not even them. He could never find the flower the clown gave him but the perfume was on his hands and in the corners of his room even after the flower had gone. No one else could smell it, no one else knew, and the others would not understand when he tried to tell. 'It's under the bed and in the curtains. It's in my Teddy. It's in my book with the lamb on the cover.

It's in the garden. It's under the house. Why is it everywhere but nowhere? Where has my flower gone?'

Its perfume was everywhere, even now; with his hands held to his face he could smell it there. With his hands taken away he could smell it there. But that happened other times, too, and in other places. One day he would find the flower and the clown would fall over and walk on his bottom and squirt water from his mouth like a hose.

No one came to take him home. People always came when he ran away. Other people always stopped and talked to him, 'Why are you lying there, little boy?' When he told them sometimes they stared or lifted him up by the hand or walked away.

'Where do you live, little boy?'

When he told them sometimes they said, 'You show us,' or 'What did he say?' or 'Can't understand a word.' Then Brenda would come puffing and blowing, or Tony, or Max, or Mummy, or Daddy.

No one came, not even to ask his name.

Not even the policeman came.

But it didn't matter because he could see the clown climbing the tiers from one level to the next with a vast red smile from one ear to the other, with a pointed cap like a steeple, with a nose shining like a knob on the end of Brenda's bed, with cheeks like a doll, with the flower held out before him.

Oh, the clown was coming up from one tier to the next, looking into his eyes. 'For you,' the clown said, and placed it in his hand, and the perfume overwhelmed him, but when he opened his palm it was not a flower that rolled away but a sticky ball like one of the marbles Tony kept in a little bag.

FOURTEEN

New World

Alison said, 'We'll see each other at weekends, won't we?'

'You bet.'

'What'll we do? Do you swim?'

'Maybe.' But he was doubtful. 'Maybe in a year or two when I'm not so thin. My ribs stick out something awful. You don't mind, do you? My ribs.'

'Of course I don't. I like boys thin, anyway. I can't stand them all sleek and silky and well fed.'

'Golly, I'm fed all right. I'm not starved. Mum says I eat like a draught horse. She reckons she's going to put me on to oats to see if it'll fatten me up. Do you swim? Do you look good in a swimsuit? Do you wear a bikini?'

She didn't answer.

'Well, do you?'

Her voice was small. 'Sometimes.'

'I bet you look beaut, too.'

'I suppose I look all right. Dad reckons I do.'

'What colour is it? Your bikini?'

'You wait and see.'

'Don't be mean. Tell me.'

She sighed. 'White. Dad always reckons white looks best.'

'So do I.'

'Well, you shouldn't. You're only fifteen.'

'Golly,' he said, 'what's wrong with fifteen? I'm not

wet behind the ears, you know. I am out of kindergarten, you know.'

'Are you?'

'Yes, I am. Lots of girls have been after me. You ask Brenda; she'll tell you.'

'So you're one of those?' (In a bantering way.)

'No, I'm not. I didn't say they caught me. I've never had a girl friend. That's true, too. I wouldn't go for any of Brenda's friends. She's fixed me for that. I pity the fellow that goes for her. She's so *bossy*. I like girls who are different.'

'But I thought you said you didn't go for girls at all?'

'Well, I don't.'

'Have you ever had a kiss?'

'Crikey,' he said, and blushed, and was glad she couldn't see.

'Well, have you?'

'No.' He wanted to sound *hurt*, but giggled instead though he tried very hard not to. 'Have *you* ever kissed a boy?'

'Not really. Only at parties. Postman's Knock and drippy things like that. But they don't count. They didn't, Max. They didn't mean anything.'

'I kissed my cousin,' he said, 'but she's eighteen. She doesn't count either. I don't suppose she can get other boys to kiss her.'

'Well, why did you do it, then?'

'I don't know. It was Christmas or something.'

'Did you like it?'

'Gee, I don't know. I suppose so. But it didn't count. Really, Alison, it didn't.'

He began to feel miserable and she heard it in his voice. 'I'm only teasing,' she said. 'I know it didn't count. But I wish I could see you, Max. I'd love to see you. You said you were dark, didn't you?'

'Black. My hair's black as coal. Everyone else in the family is fair. They reckon I'm a ring-in.'

'And you'll be six feet two.'

'I suppose so, but how can you be sure. But I won't be less than five-eleven because I'm that much now.'

'Do you think you can get me out of here?'

'I can try.'

'Because someone might come soon and then it won't be the same.'

'Who can come?' he said. 'There's no one. Only Brenda.'

'It won't be the same when she's here either, will it?'

'No.' The thought made him uncomfortable. Imagine it; trying to talk to Alison with Brenda there. Golly, with his hand in the cab, touching her head. Brenda would laugh and he'd never hear the end of it and she'd tell everyone and everything would be awful. 'No,' he said, 'I hope she doesn't come.'

'I want *you* to get me out, Max. I'd hate anyone else to do it. You do understand, don't you?'

'Yeh.'

'Go on, then. Get started.'

'You won't growl at me when I take my hand away?'

There was a soft laugh unlike any other he had ever heard and he knew that it was a very special sound; the first laugh of a girl for a boy. It could never happen again, not the same sound or the same excitement that it stirred. He laughed also, as quietly as she had, and said, 'Gee, Alison. . . .' He went quiet then and was confused.

His arm came away from the crushed cabin, almost gratefully, almost joyfully, and he sprawled on the ground stretching and flexing to hasten the circulation in his cramped limbs and had to laugh again, because laughter was the only way to cover his groans.

'Are you all right?' she said. 'You sound like someone in a dentist's chair.'

'Yeh, yeh. Maybe I do. I feel like it, too.' He creaked on to his feet and stamped around. 'I'm frozen. Golly, Alison, I'll bet you are, too.'

'I am under cover you know.'

Something about that seemed deliciously absurd and he was glad she could crack a joke because so many girls didn't know how. Getting her out of the cabin would be like flying over a mountain-top and discovering a new world.

'Max.'

'Yes.'

'Be careful, won't you. I don't mean of me; I mean of you. Watch where you put your hands. Watch what you do. There's cyanide around.'

Something about the word came out of a past almost forgotten as real. He lost a few moments when he paused and smelt the stuff again, and felt that solitary marble shoot sickeningly from his shoe. He thought of Brenda in a way he had not thought of her in an hour. 'Yeh,' he said, 'I know.' He thought of himself running down the road, and of Brenda going away alone.

'Dad was upset about it because of the dam. He didn't know how close we were. Is it far?'

'Two miles by road, but not far straight down. The road winds a couple of times. Maybe only a few hundred yards.'

'And that's bad?'

'I don't know.' He had seen the cyanide as an enemy on a front only as wide as a road. He had not thought of it in relation to the dam. 'There's an awful lot of water down there, Alison. It'd dilute it, I suppose. Make it too weak to do much harm. Kill a few fish, I suppose.'

'There's an awful lot of cyanide. Has it all gone?'

'From the trailer, you mean? Yeh, I think so.'

'Dad said there was enough to kill everyone in the State. It only takes a grain or two to kill a man.'

'Yeh, yeh, but it's not drinking water, you know. The dam's for irrigation, for farms down on the plains. Golly, there wouldn't be any shacks here if it was drinking water for a town. Anyway, the shacks are farther round.'

'No one *ever* drinks it?'

'Shouldn't think so. They're not supposed to. No one round here would drink it; we've all got rain-water tanks. Cattle drink it, though. I suppose birds do. I suppose sheep do. People might, down on the plains. You just don't know.'

'Get me out, Max.'

'O.k.'

He looked around, deliberately focussing his eyes, bringing them back from wherever they had been. He had seen nothing consciously in ages. Strange. Almost everything sensed and experienced had been in his mind, acutely alive, yet somehow he had been unaware of slope and trees and fog. *Fog that was almost gone.*

The discovery struck him with surprise. The hillside was grey with watery moonlight, with cast shadows. That stirring in the bush meant a breeze. The wreckage of the truck was stark; and above him, closer to the road, was a grotesque shape that he flinched from, from which he immediately averted his eyes, the wreckage of the car.

'Max.'

He didn't hear her. There was a thrust inside him of despair, and another thrust, of guilt. Was it right that the car should be there and Alison should be here? But none of it was of his making. It had happened that way.

'Max.'

'Yeh.'

'What's wrong?'

'Nothing; nothing. Just getting my breath. The fog's gone.'

'You can see?'

'Well enough.'

Something warned her to be satisfied with that, but something else troubled her; a feeling of insecurity; not in the way of danger but in the way of doubt. His hand was gone, as she knew it had to go, but she would never feel completely *safe* until it was back. 'What are you doing, Max?' She tried to say it casually, conversationally, but a tremor was in her voice.

Again he didn't recognize the question. He stood stiffly with hands pushed into his pockets, fingering in one pocket a two-cent coin, in the other clutching a clammy handkerchief.

'Max . . .'

'Yeh, yeh.'

'You can get me out, can't you?'

'I'm trying.'

'I can't hear you doing anything.'

It was an effort to wrench his concentration back. 'I'm trying, I'm trying. I'll have to lever the door out somehow.

Maybe that'll make an opening for you. Maybe then I'll be able to drag you through.'

'Well, do it, Max; do it.'

'I don't want to hurt you.'

'I don't care if you do.'

'It's silly to say that. I could shift something I didn't mean to. Something might fall. I could kill you.'

'Of course you won't kill me.'

'Golly, Alison; you don't see it the way I do.'

For a while it had seemed that nothing could stop him. Now it seemed there was nothing he could do. He went down on his knees against the mass of twisted metal and pushed and pulled with futility, with a helpless and weary sort of anger. 'It's *difficult*,' he sighed, 'I need tools. I'll have a look around.'

'Dad's got tools. They're in a box under the step on his side. If we're upside down they must be easy to get at.'

'I don't mean spanners and screwdrivers. I mean a dirty great lump of iron or a dirty great lump of wood. Something to lever with.'

'You'll find tyre levers there and hammers. Huge things. It's not a bicycle repair kit, you know.' Then hurriedly, almost biting her tongue, 'I'm sorry, you couldn't have known.'

But he had become silent again and his uncertainty was conveyed to her in a mysterious way; she knew that he felt beaten, she knew that he was looking around half-heartedly, almost deliberately ignoring odd pieces of bush timber that he might have used; she pictured him there, a stooped shadow with a face that could not be seen. 'There's wood about,' he said, as though answering a question clearly put, 'but it's rotten. It wouldn't take the strain. One heave and it'd split and we'd be crawling with ants and spiders and beetles. There's iron and stuff on the truck but I'd never pull it off in a million years.'

'Look in the tool box, Max. Please. It's under the step. It's part of the step on Dad's side.'

She feared his attitude of mind, the imagined expressions on his face, the fancied gestures of his hands and the colourless drone his voice had acquired. Suddenly, with astonished relief, she heard him at the other side, scrambling on the cabin with slipping shoes, and hearing him saw him vividly in her mind, a tall, thin boy with beautiful hands and black hair stretching for the tool box specially for her. But still without a face; only a shadow was there and the whites of eyes.

'I can't open it. Golly, Alison, didn't you know it was locked. There's a dirty great padlock on it.'

A weight seemed to fall; she had forgotten the lock made of case-hardened steel.

'Have you got the key?'

'Dad would have it somewhere, but heaven knows where.'

'You don't think you can find it?' It was a tired sort of call.

'How can I?'

She heard him skid back to the ground.

'Don't go, Max.'

'I'm not going anywhere. But I've got to find something to do the job with. I can't do it with my bare hands.'

'You mean you can't do it at all?'

'No, I don't mean that. Of course I'll do it. All I've got to work out is *how*.'

'Max, don't go away.'

'I haven't gone anywhere.'

He sat again beside her door.

'How do you feel?' he said.

'All right.'

'I mean, how do you really feel?'

'All right, Max. Truly. And you?'

'Golly, Alison, you ought to see it. Lying there like you are you just don't know. I think they'll have to use a crane.'

That was it; finally expressed; finally said. He would never get her out and was not going to try.

'I understand,' she said.

'Yeh.'

Shyly, then, as though it was something he shouldn't do, he found her hair again with his hand and the pressures began at once to unwind. He wanted only to breathe out, to sigh; he wanted only to close his eyes.

'Have you got a turned-up nose?' she said.

'Eh?'

'What's your nose like?'

'Golly, I don't know.'

'Where do you go to school?'

He was disconcerted by the sudden return to the questions and answers of a while ago 'I told you before.'

'No, you didn't.'

He wasn't keen to talk and sounded slightly annoyed. 'I'm sure I told you I went to Dunstan High.'

'You didn't. *Dunstan* High? Where's that?'

'In Dunstan of course.'

'There's no place called Dunstan.'

'For crying out loud, Alison; do you live in a dream? You go through Dunstan on the train on the way out to St Clare's.'

'You don't, you know. There's no place with that name.' Then he felt her alarm, felt it in his hand, in the instant that it happened in his own mind. 'Max! We're talking about the same city, aren't we? We're talking about Adelaide, aren't we?'

'Melbourne,' he said blankly. 'You *said* St Clare's.'

Her voice seemed to come from far away. 'Oh, Max, we're talking about different schools. We don't live in the same State. You're away over here; I'm away over there.'

It was like the end of an age or the end of the world.

'Oh, Max, you know what it means?'

'Yeh,' he said.

'You won't be able to call me on the phone. I won't be able to see you at weekends.'

He could have cried but said instead in a voice as deep as a man's, 'We'll find a way, Alison.'

'There isn't a way. There's nothing we can do. It's too far. It's much too far. It's five hundred miles.'

'It's not five hundred miles now, though, is it? I'm going to get you out.' He drew his hand away and said it again, 'I'm going to get you out.' Then said it again, '*I'm going to get you out.*'

FIFTEEN

A Question of Priorities

AFTER A WHILE the Fenwicks' car went slowly up through the curves on the hill, stopping and starting every few hundred yards. That was how it seemed. But then all feeling of their presence went away, there was no longer the engine faintly heard, no undecipherable voices, no suggestion of the lantern beam like an eerie cloud creeping from the road into trees. Then the forest became huge and soundless, growing minute by minute, until it reached to distances greater than the mind could see, an immensity that dismayed Brenda and Tony, that made their search seem like nothing, like a futile quest for a fragment of light among the stars, that removed David to an unknown place very far off and made them feel lost themselves, as in a way they were. Only by being together were they not lost and only by knowing that if they walked downhill they must reach the shores of the dam. They said little to each other, fearing that spoken words would end in tears. They held each other's hands and called often for David into the silence until the cry wearied.

Brenda knew David wouldn't answer because he never answered except with a chuckle or a laugh when it bubbled up for the joy of the game; and Tony knew he wouldn't answer because in the morning policemen would come all the way from Hamer with nets and chains and drag the dam the way they did in news reports when people were drowned. They'd find him then or in a few days' time, or dead in a gully somewhere higher up or farther around, or miles and miles away because there weren't any fences or houses in between.

Brenda called, 'David, David,' but knew she might step over him and not know that he was there. It was not like Luke Street at home in town. There was not the grassy verge in the sun at the side of the road where he stretched out head on ground, always in the same funny way. There were no strangers passing by with shopping baskets or prams, or friends who knew how to bring him home.

Tony called, 'Please, Fatso. Answer. I was looking after you.'

'That's silly, Tony,' Brenda said inside. 'It's got nothing to do with you. It was that stupid man. Who does he think he is? Breaking down our door. His wife's probably right. He's a drone.'

Tony thought, 'It's so cold and so wild. Gee, Fatso, what did you do it for?'

'We'll never find him,' Brenda said to herself, 'poor little kid without any shoes or clothes. Only his pyjamas. He'll freeze.'

Then Brenda thought, 'Isn't it strange? First Mum and Dad then David straight away. Almost as if Mum knew. Almost as if she said, "There's no one to look after you now. You'd better come along with me."'

Tony said out loud, 'Gee, sis; have we done the right thing? Should we have scooted off from the Fenwicks the way we did? We can't see enough. The torch is no good. If we've lost him what are we going to tell Mum and Dad?'

Brenda called, 'Where are you, David? It's Brenda and Tony to take you home, to tuck you back into bed.'

But when she got him home, really home, back in town, what would she do? She couldn't leave school to look after him; it wasn't fair; she'd not be fifteen until next year; only fifteen even then and she wanted to stay on two years more for matriculation. And later she wanted to go on to college to be a teacher, not remain nursemaid to a Mongoloid child. She wanted to be somebody, not a drudge like Mum trotting backwards and forwards to the Training Centre with David every day. Unless she taught David and other kids like him and made that her career. 'Golly, Dad, you should have thought. Fancy getting killed. What a stupid thing to do. All these years you've been driving a car. All those years you flew in a plane. What did you go and do it for?' She recalled what Gran had said last time she came: 'Drive out of that bend like that again, my man, and I'll take to you with a stick no matter how old you are. Do you want to kill yourself and everyone else too? Haven't you any sense?'

Tony thought, 'Oh, I wish Mum and Dad were here. Then everything would be right as rain. Mrs Fenwick's so sure they're held up somewhere on the road. They've just *got* to be held up somewhere.'

Brenda thought, 'Not a sign of him, but how would we see if there were? All this fog drifting about; all these trees; all these ups and downs. Every blooming rock he could be lying behind and I'd never know. David, answer me. Max will be frantic up there on his own.'

Tony thought, 'We'll never find him. I know.'

Brenda said to herself, 'I wish I knew the time. I can't add up the hours any more; it seems like years. Is it five o'clock? Six? Surely it'll be light soon. Have I ever wished for day as I wish for it now?'

'It's my fault,' Tony sobbed inside, 'it's all my fault for being a coward and forgetting that Fatso was there. Max asked me to look after him and I promised. Poor little Fatso, where have you gone?'

Frank Fenwick stopped the car for the tenth or eleventh time. 'We'll try again,' he said, explaining the obvious, and stepped on to the road. 'You go downhill. I'll go up.'

'Frank.' His wife's call was reproachful.

'What is it now? Hasn't it all been said?'

'Why don't you drive on to the bend? Why keep putting it off? You won't face facts.'

'It's got nothing to do with putting anything off, but everything to do with *facing* facts.'

'You're scared of what you'll find.'

He knew he should have walked away but he stayed. It had never been different; always wanting to get away from her, but always staying. 'Phyllis; it's a question of priorities.'

'You said that before.'

'I'll say it again. The priorities haven't changed. The child comes first. He'd never have got out if I hadn't broken the door. You live with your conscience; I'll live with mine. What's happened at the bend has nothing directly to do with me. The child has everything to do with me.'

'You're scared.'

'Oh, for pity's sake. *Scared?* Who isn't? Aren't you?'

'The eldest Shaw boy is up there on his own. You must be close enough to call.'

'He's made his choice; good luck to him. I've made mine. I dare not get involved up there. It's got to be one thing at a time.'

Again he should have walked away, but again he stayed.

'You must be close enough, Frank, to blow the horn. He'd surely hear. I'm worried for that boy.'

'Meaning I'm not! You're the expert with the horn. You blow it. But when you blow it don't count on me.'

'Frank.' Again she sounded hurt, but with her a man could never be sure.

'It's too late, Phyllis. The damage is done. Your tongue got us into this but it won't get us out of it. We needed those children down there, young Tony and Brenda, as they needed us. You played to your audience but you lost it. So now there are two of us to do the searching instead of four. Kids never were your cup of tea. They don't like your style. You go downhill; I'll go up.'

He walked away, the point scored, but not as positive at heart as he might have seemed, nowhere near as angry with her as his words implied, not even certain that his own sense of what had to come first was as genuine as hers. At heart he was an honest man; on the surface he wore a mask and changed his mask with mood. Yes; he was scared. Yes; he was putting off the mess at the bend until it was there, presented to him, no longer possible to avoid. He knew he'd face it when it came, but he thought, 'let's not face it while we have another script to read; this other script is real; there are no ifs or buts about the retarded boy.'

What were these kids to do if their parents were dead? There was more to it than met the eye. Shaw had been an airman in the war. Kids of ex-servicemen were not ignored. Guardians would be found. Maybe a housekeeper would be put into their home. They'd be seen through school. They'd not be destitute. Shaw was not poor and his kids were a ready-made family for someone to own. It was a thought to sleep on. For two pins he'd stake a claim, except for the retarded boy. There was something about retardation that sickened him inside and there was something about Phyllis that kids couldn't stand. They knew, somehow, that she didn't care. What were these kids to do with the retarded boy? Maybe he'd be better in the dam; maybe he'd be better not found. Living half a life was worse than no life at all; not even half a life; nothing but a shade; a body and impulses and no comprehension of the world around. Stick him in an institution with all the other vegetables growing there. He'd seen an institution once, for a full working day, filmed it, set in beautiful countryside. In the car afterwards, with the rest of the team on the way back to town, he wept and no one asked him why.

Then he paused at the edge where the road fell away, aware that at some recent moment he had walked out of the fog as if he had walked out of a room. He looked back for the car but couldn't see it. Still enough fog back there to soak up the parking lights, or had he come farther than he supposed, or had there been a curve in the road? Was there a breeze, the faintest of breezes, like ice, on his face? Was there a smell, sweet and somehow unwholesome, as if it were a smell better left on its own. Was it cyanide? Was *that* the smell of cyanide?

He shivered.

It was the straight stretch of road below the bend and he had walked on to it before he knew, committing himself before he was ready. Almost guiltily he switched off the lantern and sank into a darkness for which he was not prepared. Lantern light had dazzled him, bruised his eyes. But it was not totally dark after all. There was moonlight of a kind like a grey film. Three hundred yards to the bend, no more. The eldest Shaw boy was up there. Heaven alone knew what else was there.

He strained to see and hear in detail, but was frustrated by recurring ghosts of the lantern beam and by the dulling effect of cold. But there were details just the same, of sight and sound; lumps on the road close by, noises like creatures in the undergrowth farther off, and an overpowering sense of tragedy that seemed to possess every leaf and tree and breath of air.

'It's happened all right. What the girl says is true.'

The words were spoken aloud and he listened to himself as he would hear another person whose opinion he respected.

The lumps on the road were cyanide drums. The noises farther off must have been the boy, that eldest boy all alone with a job on hand that would daunt a man, that daunted this man. The urge to get back from the edge of the road was irresistable; the fear of seeing made him turn his head. He stepped back and looked directly into the ditch, directly at something there that was neither drum nor rock nor wood.

'My God.'

It was the little boy.

The call that rose up was weak with shock—from how the child lay and even from finding him when he had not expected that he would. Then he was beside the boy, reaching down, fearing deeply the touch that he knew had to come back to him through his hands. Cold. The boy was cold and face-down. As cold as the man's hands were, the boy was colder still, and every nerve of his body recoiled. Dead, dead, dead he was sure. Forty years of age and he had never seen a lifeless human being before. 'Oh, my God,' he said, 'what do I do? His life is on me.'

Around him was the smell of death, of cyanide, and he drew back, looking down, and switched on the lantern beam. It was a small blue-clad boy down there, arms and feet bare, pyjamas torn, blood-stained, sparkling with dew, with repulsive marbles of potassium cyanide, sticky and glazed, not twelve inches from his head.

It was horrible, fascinating, unutterably sad, and to put the light on him in the way that he did, almost brutally, was a dreadful invasion of privacy. You didn't turn brilliant lights on the dead, you covered them with a sheet or a blanket or a coat. Oh yes, you did. Ashamed, he allowed the lantern light to drift to one side as though he had intended all along not to direct it downwards as he had, then he slipped out of his coat aware in a different way of intense cold, coldness not of the air but of his own flesh internally, at depth. Then the boy moved.

Frank Fenwick stifled a gasp, almost of terror, dropped the lantern, dropped the coat, and sickened to a bitter sting in his throat.

'David,' he said, and scooped him up from the ditch, pressing him to his chest, cradling him there, crushing him with emotion, willing the heat of his own blood into the body of the boy. 'Oh, David,' he said, 'bless you for being alive. Oh, David, David; what would I have done if you had been dead?'

He walked, unable to stand still, burning with the heat he tried to give to the boy. 'Come back, David, don't go away. If it's cyanide in you let it pass into me. God, if you're real, hear me. If anyone can care for kids like this it's got to be You. If You let these things happen You've got to carry some of the load.'

The boy was like ice against his chest, a block of ice with a heartbeat, not stirring against the pressure of the arms that hugged him. Was it cyanide in him? Was it only cold? If cyanide was there was it less than lethal? No one would ever know. It would kill if it was going to before anyone could get it out. You could never get cyanide out. Never, almost never was there time. He crushed the boy tighter, longing for him to struggle, to kick or fight or claw, but if there was an awareness in the boy of anything at all it was only of warmth. The heartbeat inside him pulsed against the warmth, pulsed inside the warmth like a tiny coal in the heart of a fire.

Frank Fenwick, with something like shock, saw the road, and instantly felt that he had walked much too far the wrong way; perhaps for the first time realized fully that the scene had changed, that the lantern he had dropped was no longer at his feet, that he was even walking at all.

He had almost reached the bend!

There it was; not a hundred and fifty yards; vague, dark with night and its associations in his mind; the bend, the deep furrow, and wreckage strewn on the road. Noises, too, came to him from below, over the side. Sensing them there, he confused his hearing to shut them out, and, in the stride that registered his understanding of where he was, deliberately pivoted on the sole of his shoe to face the other way.

He didn't care what was down there; he didn't want to know. The priority was in his arms. Get involved down there over the side and David might die. To get life back into the bundle in his arms was all that mattered now. He pivoted, he hurried away, a decision of an instant because he was afraid; but then in his brain something snapped into vision seconds after he had seen it with his eyes; a broken board, a painted sign, torn, he supposed, from the cyanide truck that had plunged into disastrous depths. 'SPEED IT THRU MAC'.

How could he have seen such a thing? How could he have read it? Were they words in the dark, written down, or a spoken voice?

He hurried away, clinging to David; almost stumbling with haste.

SPEED IT THRU MAC.

He had imagined it, not seen it, and the harder he thought back the more indistinct it became. It had not been there. It was in his mind, an unoriginal and faintly silly phrase, a shadow of things forgotten shaken up by shock and fear into recent levels of memory where it did not belong; meaning nothing; having nothing to do with the present at all. The present was David Shaw, a small, soft, sub-normal child clutched to him and clutching back.

In a moment that was almost delirious he felt fingers at the cloth of his shirt, a spasm of life like a shudder.

'David!'

Every shred of the man's will and attention turned towards the boy. 'Come on, David; come on, David. Wake up.'

But the spasm had gone.

'Wake up!'

But he was soft and limp and cold again, even though the heartbeat pulsed in the warmth wrapped around. 'Don't go on me now, boy. Whatever you do, don't go now.'

Was it the last flutter of life going? . . . The heartbeat was still there.

He hurried again, stumbling from haste, weak in the legs, and the lantern with its beam was still where he had left it on the road. The coat too, that was there; and the recollection of David face-down in the ditch was there also. He held the boy close, giving him warmth, but still could see him as he had been, dead in the ditch. Dead down there, but alive in his arms. Which was real? Or was everything imagined like that silly phrase in the dark?

The sign must have been there or else why would it have appeared? What, in the experience of this night, could resurrect words like those without direct and visible cause?

With the lantern and his coat and the boy he headed back for the car, not able to foresee what he would do, but in his heart he knew he was already running away.

'Phyllis,' he would say, 'you mustn't go up there. It's not the place for you. Don't ask me why. I can't explain. Instinct, if you like. Yes, call it that. If you were a nurse, my dear, it would be a different thing. An emotional woman like you would fall apart. Emotional? Dare I call her that. She's as hard as nails. Not that nails are without their special qualities; not that Phyllis is without hers. We've got to get back to the house. Phyllis. We've got to get this kid warm. Hot-water bottles. Stoke up the fire. We've got to get salt water down him somehow to make him sick. Just in case, you know. Or maybe milk. What do you do with cyanide, Phyllis? I thought it killed you quick, like a knife, but he's still hanging on. It could be pneumonia, Phyllis. Hospital, do you think? Should we run him through to Hamer? But if it's cyanide he'll be dead before we're there. In conditions like this it'll take hours. How do we get round the bend? All that rubbish to shift. My God, you go to bed at night and you just never know what'll happen before dawn.'

She was there. She was at the car (misted, but plain), leaning on an elbow as if all the patience in the world resided in her, but he couldn't produce a voice to call. His back was aching now from the weight; his breath was short; he was trembling from head to toe.

What was he to say? How was he to keep her away from up there? The sign must be real; he *couldn't* have imagined anything as personal as that, as close to home as *Speed it Thru Mac*, as close to Phyllis as the man whose wife she had been ten years ago. He was a man with a grievance, Phyllis had said, with an eye on her money and an eye on her fame. He'd turn up one day, she'd said; after all, a woman in the public eye would not be hard to track down.

'He has no right. You're divorced. It's finished.'

'No right,' she had said, 'none at all. But he was a *little* man with a *little* mind. He was *small*. All brawn, no brain.'

Her arm dropped from the car, she called, she started his way. He stumbled towards her neither walking nor running, but hastening unsteadily.

'You've found him,' she said. 'Oh, Frank. How wonderful.'

He brushed past her, believing in the rightness of his urge to turn the car about (somehow) and drive home. Turning on that road? How? How? 'He's ill, he's ill,' he said. 'We must hurry. I don't know whether it's cyanide or cold.'

He leant against the car, panting, shaking with nerves, aware that his words had been slurred and probably not understood.

She was behind him. 'Is he dead?'

'Sick, sick. Into the car quickly. You nurse him. We must get him home.'

'Frank, quieten down. You're frightening me.'

'There are things to be frightened about. Get in the car.'

She moved to his order, surprising him (he had expected argument) and he passed David into her arms. 'Wouldn't it be better if I drove,' she said. 'You're in such a state.'

He slid into the car and clung to the steering-wheel. It was wonderful to sit down. 'Oh, Phyllis,' he said.

But she had forgotten him for the moment, had switched on the inside light and with a handkerchief moistened with saliva was wiping David's face, David so awkwardly held in her lap. 'Pretty,' she said. 'Like a doll. What was that you said? Where did you find him?'

'Cyanide,' he said breathlessly.

'Nonsense.'

'It was all around him.'

'They tell me these children *know* about these things.'

He stared at her.

'Yes,' she said. 'Really.'

He shook his head. 'It's a fairy-tale. They don't know about cyanide. How could they? I don't know about it myself. These children don't know anything.'

'If he'd eaten cyanide he'd be dead.'

'We must make sure. Salt and water. We've got to get it into him.' He started the engine but her right hand came over and rested on his arm. 'You're in an awful hurry.'

'Wouldn't you be?'

'No. No, I wouldn't be. This child's not poisoned. If he were he'd show some sign.'

'He's frozen. Exhausted. You didn't see him when I picked him up.'

'No,' she said, 'I didn't. But he's all right, Frank.'

'You don't know. You're guessing. You can't guess about life or death.'

'He's all right, Frank. Take a deep breath. Look for yourself. I wouldn't say so unless he were. Where did you find him?'

'In the ditch.'

'I mean *where*?'

'Up there somewhere.' He couldn't hide it from her; he couldn't. She always knew.

'It was near the bend, wasn't it? You've got to face it, Frank. The priority has changed. You can't shelter behind this little boy. Don't make out he's sicker than he is. Don't fill him up with poisons that aren't there. He's safe now. He's all right now. You've found him and that was well done.'

'We can't be sure.'

'I *am* sure. I get surer every moment. Don't run away, Frank, and spoil it.'

'You don't understand. You don't know what you're talking about.'

'There's not much about you that I don't understand.'

'Oh, Phyllis.' At heart he was in despair. She didn't understand; she only thought she did.

'I'll go with you,' she said. 'Death doesn't worry me as it worries you.'

'It's no place for you up there. Allow me to know.'

'What are you hiding?'

'*Nothing.*'

'Very well, then. I'll stay in the car. I'll keep David warm. You go. You must go, Frank. It's not only now. You'll have to live with tonight for the rest of your life.'

His head drooped over the wheel and he easily could have given way. 'There are things you don't know.' It was at the point of pouring out; it almost choked him to hold it back.

'What is it, Frank?'

Nothing came. Not a word.

'All right,' she said, 'I appreciate your concern for my feelings, but you can't leave the Shaw boy in a situation like that on his own.' She almost said, 'Be a man'; it was so close to her lips that he heard it as clearly as if it had been spoken aloud.

But he didn't drive forward; he started backing down. 'The little boy could be dying, Phyllis, and you just don't care. There are the other children to find, too. The living, Phyllis, before the dead.'

SIXTEEN

The Opposite Face

MAX PROWLED ROUND the wreck at a distance of several yards like an angry young lion, eyeing it from different angles, determined to crack it like a nut if he had to, to get Alison out. He'd take it apart with his bare hands if he had to. He'd pull her out, he'd drag her out, gently, to show her the sky, to let her breathe the air, to say, 'Here I am.' To think, 'There you are.' To sigh, 'Where do we go from here? I'm younger than Romeo but you're just right for Juliet.'

How could a fellow say things like that! It was drippy. It wasn't, you know.

Brenda would laugh her silly-looking head off. Blow Brenda.

Tony would say, 'A *girl*.' As if she was something like an earwig or a horrible-looking grub. Tony could go fly a kite.

Mum and Dad would say. . . . What would Mum and Dad have said? Mum would have gone into orbit, 'Max! You're much too young.' Dad would have said, 'When I was your age, son—' Then he would have looked at Alison again. 'I don't know; if these things happen to a *man* I guess he can't be too young.'

But the slope was so steep in spots Max had to move on all fours, had to cling to scrub, had to hang on to rocks, dislodging cascades of stones with his feet. It was a shocking place. 'I can't believe she's in there. I can't believe she's alive. You are there, Alison, aren't you?'

'Of course I am. Where else could I be? Have you found anything yet?'

He clambered over the upturned trailer from end to end (dirty, oily, treacherous thing), wrenching and heaving at every plank and length of iron partly broken away until he was filthy and frantic and his senses seemed to be rushing off in all directions at once. Something *had* to snap; something had to give. She was down there in the middle of that ghastly mess, only inches out of reach. It wasn't fair, it was all wrong. It was like being outnumbered by about five to one in a fight, by opponents all twice his size and himself fighting for something worth the world. But nothing gave except splinters, nothing snapped off that he could use, nothing long enough to manipulate or strong enough to bear a desperate pressure, the sort of pressure he would be putting on to get Alison out. Terrific pressure, veins standing up in knots, strength like a man's, with groaning metal bending, resisting grimly, finally giving way. Then out she'd come, 'Max, Max; you're so strong.'

Alison called, 'Have you found anything yet?'

'I'm looking,' he said, 'I won't be long.' But the tension he heard in her voice was the same tension that he felt in himself, as if they were living where everything was wild and dark, as if everyone else in the world lived far away in the light, as if they alone were condemned to exist in isolation.

Her cry came again, 'Have you found anything yet?'

'Gee, Alison. Give me a chance.'

He squatted on the bottom of the trailer, foolishly hugging an axle housing, initially to rest on it, but then to plead with it to separate into its components, but knowing perfectly well that only a man with gas cylinders and torches would cut through it, knowing that if by some miraculous accident chance released it for him he would be saddled with a monstrous lump of metal too heavy to move. But he pulled and tugged and pleaded until the emotion that drove him drained out. He groaned against the axle, hating the rotten thing because it had beaten him, because it had never intended to give in, because it was there and had made a fool of him.

Alison called again, 'Don't, Max. Don't carry on. Don't hurt yourself like that.'

'I'll get you out,' he hissed, 'I will, I will.'

'If you can't, you can't. There's no disgrace. If you're not strong enough you can't help it.' She knew it was the wrong thing to say but she meant it with all her heart.

'I *am* strong enough.'

'You can't be, Max,' she said. 'You're not a man and I wouldn't want you to be. I don't expect you to do it. I'm not asking you to do it, not now I'm not. I said before that I understood.'

'I don't care what you said. I've got to get you out.'

'You said before only a crane could shift it. Look, Max; I don't mind waiting. We've got to wait. It's no one's fault.'

'You're not going to wait.' But he knew she'd have to. 'I'm going to get you out.' But he knew he wouldn't. 'I'll get something from somewhere to do it with.' But he knew there was nothing.

'What about the car then? Can't you get something from there?'

'*No.*'

'Why not?'

'*No.*'

He let go of the axle and lay there, empty.

'Max. There are still the tools in my Dad's box.'

Her words seemed idle now, and inconsequential, words simply for the sake of words.

'Did you hear me? There's still Dad's tool-box.'

He sighed. 'You know it's locked.'

'You could smash it. You could throw a rock at it.'

Something stirred in him, a faint point of interest, the germ of a question or of a challenge or perhaps of hope, and that awful feeling of helplessness, of not being strong enough presented, suddenly (almost thunderously), its opposite face. 'Yes,' he shouted, 'by golly, yes.' He heaved himself up, sprawled over the edge of the trailer and there were rocks everywhere, beautiful rocks as heavy as cannon balls, so many perfect rocks that he kept picking them up and dropping each in favour of another, so excited that he almost lost track of what he was doing, until he found himself scrambling on to the cabin somewhere above Alison's head.

'Have you got one?'

'Yeh, yeh.'

It was a lump of basalt that he had and he brought it down with a karate-like blow on the bottom of the box. It jarred him to his teeth, hit him like a kick in the neck. Then, like a forgotten thought, the rock fell from his numbed fingers to fall somewhere; he neither heard it nor felt it go, thudding, rolling, crackling through sticks. He groaned into the depths of his body but didn't make a sound.

'Did you get it? Did it break?'

He couldn't answer. There was nothing in his brain but stars.

'Max?'

Half-heartedly, he tried to answer, but couldn't. He needed all the air he could get. All he really wanted was to be sick.

'You've hurt yourself. Oh, Max, what have you done?'

His grunt told her nothing.

'You didn't *hammer* it, did you? I said *throw* it. Oh, Max, you haven't broken your hand!'

What a horrible thought! He looked at his hands, as much as he could see of them through his stars, and turned them over almost expecting them to drop off, and for no reason that made sense suddenly wanted to laugh, but that sound, too, was unidentifiable and she thought he was sobbing. She struggled in her sharp prison, thwarted almost beyond endurance because she couldn't see him. 'For heaven's sake, Max,' she wailed, 'why don't you tell me what you've done?'

'I hammered it,' he groaned. 'I didn't think. I'm stupid. It couldn't have hurt more if I'd hit it with my head.'

'Oh you have. You've broken your hand. You've broken that beautiful hand.'

'*No!* I didn't say I'd broken it.'

'You did, you just did.'

'I didn't and I haven't,' he shrilled, 'what *beautiful* hand, anyway?'

He could hear her draw breath. 'The one you put on my head.'

'Ugh.' That sounded real wet, but he peered at his right hand again, blinking almost owlishly, and with effort managed to move his fingers.

'Seems to be all right,' he said, more to himself than to her. But beautiful? Maybe in a way it was, in a special way that he was sure he would never forget but would never be able to explain to another living soul. 'Yeh,' he said, now not sickened as much, with fewer stars. 'You know, I've been seeing stars. I dunno when I saw them last. When I was about eight, I reckon. When I fell off the monkey bars and got a green-stick fracture.'

'You've got a green-stick fracture!'

'No, no, no. When I was *eight.*'

'Max, I wish you'd talk sense. You're wearing me out. I don't know what you're talking about half the time. I can't see you. It's awfully hard trying to guess.'

He sighed. 'Yeh. You're not telling me a thing. It's hard just having to guess.' (He guessed that she was pretty.) Then his voice suddenly went up the scale. 'Hey,' he said, 'hey, Alison. The tool-box isn't iron. It's only wood. It's split across the bottom.' (Then he guessed again, gloriously, a wildly elated guess like a flash of light; saw himself getting her out; saw himself drawing her out head and shoulders first through a gap in the side most wonderfully made by his strength; saw himself saying, 'Hello, Alison.' And there she was.)

His heels were jammed against the split in the box and he was bracing himself and pushing with every muscle, sinew and bone he could bring to bear, scarcely hearing her words beating up from below. 'Hit it again, why don't you? Drop another rock on it. Get down and get another rock.' But he thrust with his heels into the split until the pulse in his head brought back the stars and the box suddenly cracked. His own pressure set free in an instant shot him yelping over the edge and dumped him on the ground on his back. His yelp became a gust of air punched out, of speechless surprise.

He could hear her calling him, but he contracted on to his side, curving and gasping, possessed by laughter rather than moans, and rolled on to something hard that dug into his ribs. It felt like a stone but it wasn't. Then it felt like a hammer and it was. He started groping in a stunned, astonished way and there were tools everywhere, spanners and screwdrivers, oil cans, tyre levers and nuts and bolts. They had fallen behind him and around him. They should have struck him. They should have killed him. The hammer must have fallen like a pound of lead.

He pushed himself to a sitting position, creaking in every bone, hazily aware of rocks on the ground and of other hard and sharp things that should have killed him when he fell. He sobered and groaned to Alison, 'I'm still alive, by the skin of me teeth . . .'

'Do you really think you should?' she said.

'Eh?'

'You're going to hurt yourself, I think. I'd rather you didn't try.'

'Didn't try what?'

'I think you must be accident-prone or something.'

'Crumbs,' he said, 'who's talking? Look; I've got the tools—'

'That's something you didn't need to say. I reckon everyone in miles knows that!'

'I've got the tools and I'm going to use them—as soon as I can drag me bones into a working heap and get them off the ground.' Then he thought about it, about the way he had expressed it, and was surprised and pleased by his own wit, but Alison said, 'Don't you think you've hurt yourself enough?'

'Look; do you want to get out—or don't you?'

'Of course I want to get out.'

'All right, then. Let it go at that.'

Again he heard the intake of her breath, but she didn't

answer and he felt a little older and a little stronger because she hadn't. And in his imagination saw the wonderful gap open up wide in the side of the wreck, saw her waiting there, saw her smiling, saw her face changing as though a master magician was producing an illusion, but all were faces that he had seen before on other people. She was all the girls he had ever known; she was Brenda, she was cousin Jenny, she was the girl in the train, every girl noticed on the street, every girl known at school; all of them in one. It was confusing. But into his numbed hands he was gathering the largest screwdrivers, the tyre levers, and the bulbous hammer, the keys that might open the door on to the one girl he had not seen, the girl who was only a voice and a head of hair. This, too, was confusing. Suddenly, he was bothered because everything seemed to be grotesque.

'Max!'

She knew. She knew. Every time he drifted off she called him in the same way.

'I'm coming,' he said, but was not wholly sure that he wanted to. Something about the hole in the side not opened yet, was beginning to frighten him.

'Max. What's wrong?'

He stumbled round the front of the wreck, hugging the tools, slipping on the slope, with a curious tremble building up in his limbs and the pit of his stomach. When he got to the door he folded weakly on to his knees and spilled the tools with a metallic clatter into a heap and when he tried to speak he couldn't. The tremble possessed even his voice.

He knelt there, shaking, only a foot or two from her, trying to relax, to master himself, to conceal from her the dismaying turmoil of his senses and emotions. But he couldn't; she knew all the time, though not understanding it any more than he did. The strange sounds she could hear from him, the murmurings, the sharp and irregular breathing, were qualities she recognized in her own nervousness, things that had not happened to her, but had almost happened, were constantly there never more than a moment short of breaking through to the surface. She had to leave him to it, she couldn't help, because deep down she knew she was the cause. But the longer she endured it with him the thinner her own control became, the quicker her pulse, the sharper her breathing.

Max lost minutes from time and memory simply kneeling there, almost like a pilgrim at the end of a journey of years. Inches away was the object of his journey, a holy mystery, the other face of sadness. Then his fingers felt the crushed and crinkled cabin and traced the edge of the door until he felt it bulging outward. Somehow he said, 'O.k., Alison. I'm going to try.' Almost overwhelmed by the moment, he twisted the end of the tyre lever between the bulge of the door and the frame and unsteadily cracked it home an inch or two with the hammer. Then he put a trial strain on it and it held.

Slowly, he gathered his strength with deep breaths and bore hard against the side of the cabin, shortened the reach of his legs parallel to it and worked the heels of his shoes into the ground. Little by little he applied more weight to the lever until the pressure lifted his body. A great gulp of air momentarily stilled his shaking and he wrenched with all the strength he dared apply, fearing that the lever might break free of its seating and pitch him backwards into torn and jagged metal. He could have sworn that the tyre lever bent, that the door peeled outwards, but nothing budged an inch. He slumped exhausted, expelling breath, almost sick with his shaking.

In a minute or two he tried again, failed again, collapsed again.

When Alison spoke he was surprised to hear a voice that stammered like his own. 'Third time lucky, but then no more.'

'D'you reckon we ought to pray?'

'No!' She was breathless. 'If it didn't work, who'd we blame?'

He heaved himself up on the lever, trying to pivot outwards on his heels, away from danger, then everything happened as he had foreseen. Anger, impatience and absolute recklessness flared. The pulse in his head threw up stars, his veins knotted and every atom of strength absorbed since the day he was born came up with the heat. Something cracked, something gave with an appalling shock, and he threw himself frantically sideways and crashed against the ground. There he lay, panting, blinded with giddiness, terrified that everything had crumbled, that Alison had been crushed.

He tried to listen for her above the roaring in his head; then he raised himself and crawled back to the door. 'Alison . . .'

He was astonished, for suddenly grasping at him was a hand.

SEVENTEEN

Boys go Away

MAX COULD SEE the hand faintly in the dark like an extra-ordinary plant feverishly growing out of the earth, with tentacles desperate for light and sustenance. It unnerved him. It was impossible to associate with Alison anything other than a voice and a head. The hand was like another dimension or another person; it seemed a separate living thing. He wanted to draw back from it, to escape, but couldn't. He was held somewhere between horror and fascination, while the hand groped and grabbed, perhaps searching for his own fingers. Then it found them and closed over them and charged him with an electrifying shock.

That hand was as cold as anything of flesh he had ever felt and it stirred in him a deep compassion, an overflowing, and he wrapped it about with warmth, pressing it between his own hands hot from labour and sweat. Then her other hand, not seen by him, fastened on his wrist and there weren't any more thoughts, nothing but silence and a sense of contact like mountain tops.

He came back from his heights to hear her voice, very small and shy and nervous. 'Max, I've turned over. I've undone my safety-belt. I'm facing your way. Do you think there's enough light?'

Oh, he knew what she meant but he was frightened; was there enough light to see by; was there enough light to turn heads and hands and voices into faces?

Oh, he was frightened. His face might not please her. She might go quiet and remote.

'Max, I'm not very pretty. Do you mind?'

'I'm not very handsome.'

'I've got a weak chin.'

'I don't care. I'm no oil painting either. Brenda's got all the looks in our family, except for her freckles.'

Then she said, 'Max, let's get it over.'

'Faces don't matter, you know. They don't, Alison.'

'Of course they don't. I don't care what you look like. I know what you are.'

He was almost in a panic. 'Let's not look, eh? I'll get you out first. Then we'll know. Gee, Alison; it's silly; but I can't get my breath.'

'Things in here have shifted,' she said, 'they scared me half to death; but they haven't shifted enough for you to get me out.'

'Shall I try? Let me try. I wanted so much to say hullo.'

'If you try again, Max, things might shift another way and make it worse.'

'Oh, gee,' he said, struggling for breath. 'I'm not very clean, Alison. I'm terribly dirty. My hair's all over the place.'

After a while she said, 'I'm covered in sick.'

Everything that he felt turned into a sigh. 'All right . . .' And the pressure of her grasp relaxed, their hands unlocked, and he flattened on the ground and peered into the wreckage. Inside it was black. Nothing was recognizable. The things he had seen before when he had first glimpsed her hair seemed not to be there any more. Nothing seemed to be there except darkness, not even her hands after she had drawn them back.

With a start that made his heart jump he sensed a face, much, much closer than the depths he had been searching.

'Hullo, Max.'

He couldn't speak.

'I like you,' she said. 'I think you're lovely.'

He saw the white of eyes and a face forming about them,

line by line, shape by shape, something fainter and harder to piece together than any picture he had ever drawn.

'You don't eat enough carrots,' she said.

'What have carrots got to do with it?'

'Isn't that what the pilots used to eat in the war? So they could see in the dark?'

Around the movement of her lips the face was momentarily there, indescribably pale, a girl's face but a woman's face, then it fell apart, line by line and shape by shape, and was gone.

'It's too dark,' he cried, 'I can't see.'

'You're very serious about things, Max, aren't you?'

But her face was in his mind. Nothing like Brenda. Nothing like the girl in the train. But like Mum as she used to be long ago before Max was born, in the photograph on Dad's study wall, Mum at eighteen peeping coyly through apple blossom on a spring day. (Dad's explanation: 'I'd just kissed her. Can't you see?') No, not like that; how could it have been; but what else would have accounted for his unexpected calm?

'You can see me, can't you?' she said.

'No. It's too dark. And I don't think you can see me either.'

She didn't answer.

He reached in and found her nose, surprisingly not where he had expected it to be, then moved his hand gently back to her hair with an odd sense of well-being, with a feeling that he had come to a moment of understanding not to be trifled with. 'Alison. Tell me who I look like?'

He could feel her shaking under his hand.

'I'm like your Dad, aren't I?'

She suddenly sobbed.

'I'm glad,' he said, overwhelmed by the mystery, 'because now I reckon a lot of awfully funny things make sense to me.' He had to hunt for words; they didn't come pouring out; they even tangled his tongue as they came. 'I don't think we really have to see each other, you know that? I don't think it'll matter if we never see each other.' He could feel her shaking, just as he had been shaking before.

'I don't know what I would have done tonight if it hadn't been for you. I don't know how I'd have got round to facing up to what's ahead of me, but I reckon I can handle it now, honest I do.'

'No, Max, no. What are you saying?'

'Gee, Alison, it's plain enough, isn't it?'

'It's plain all right. It's too plain for me. You sound like a crummy old man.'

'Hey,' he said, deeply hurt, 'fair go.'

'You take one look at my face and before you can catch your breath you're talking about going away.'

'But I didn't see you. I couldn't have done.'

'I don't believe you.'

He wailed, 'Look, I'm talking about something else altogether, not about going away. This horrible bloomin' accident, that's what I'm talking about. It's not the end of everything, it's not the end of the world. Things sort of go on but take a new turn. It's just got to make sense to you; it does to me. I was looking at my mother. You looked just like her to me.'

'Well, maybe I do. Who's to say I shouldn't? Who's to say I don't?'

'That's silly.' Irritation rose up, almost like bile. 'You *couldn't* look like her any more than I could look like your Dad.'

Something seemed to shrink beneath his hand, almost as if Alison herself were becoming smaller. 'Max,' she said, 'don't leave me here.'

'Why should I do that?'

'Don't just pack up and walk away, will you?'

'Crikey! What the heck do you think I am?'

'Girls say things like that, Max, because it's what happens all the time. Girls say it's different with boys. It's true, too. You're saying awful things to me.'

He drew back from her, away from the wreckage, quite dismayed. Then he shrilled at her, 'What sort of words have I got to put it in? I thought I was saying something good. I thought I was facing up to facts, living in different cities and all, not being able to see each other at weekends.

Have I got to say I'll marry you when we grow up or something?'

'You'll never do that. Nothing's surer than that. You're going away.' Then she cried and Max didn't understand, he didn't, he didn't. Maybe it was a woman in there, not a girl, or a creature from another planet where people used the same language, but had different meanings for all the words. 'Alison,' he wailed. 'Don't cry. Be fair.'

Then curiously, uneasily, and instantaneously, he felt as if this struggle were not private at all, but a public performance, as if people were looking on; a conviction that the most personal hour of his life had, by accident, been transported to a stage. His desperation took a sudden and different turn and its urgency got through to her as if there had been not a moment of conflict between them. '*Someone's here!*'

She stifled herself, perhaps even thrust her knuckles into her mouth. A gasp cut her crying short.

Max's hair bristled and the night was darker than it had been at any other time. The moon had gone. Perhaps even fog was there. Trees were there, blacker than black. A breeze was there, rustling. Perhaps this was that hour before dawn! Cold was there, too, with rawness and intensity. Something led him to search the face of his watch (a suspicion that perhaps days had passed), but its luminosity had paled and made no sense. Then something urged him on to his feet and a startling sensation about his ankles, a tingling of blood, felt like Alison's breath issuing at ground level from the wreck.

'Who's there?' It was his own voice, but so hoarse he wondered whether the words were back-to-front. His cheeks were flaming and his eyes were smarting, suddenly burning up with the fear that someone had overheard; what passed between Alison and himself was not for another living ear, for *no one*. 'Is anybody there?'

How could there be anyone else? How could there be another soul on the earth apart from Alison and himself? Not even Brenda was real any more. Not even Tony. Not even David. All were abstracts, part of a former life, of an imagined life that used to be. A whisper moved about his feet. 'Is anyone there?'

It welled up in Max, wildly, a yell that rang in his own ears, '*Who's there?*'

A beam of light dazzled him as if bending from the sky, swept across the boles of trees, back and forth across wreckage and flayed scrub, and locked on to him with a grip that he could feel, that he loathed, that he wanted to run away from, but it held him transfixed, with eyes shut, with arms shielding them.

'Oh, Max . . . Someone's here.'

'Max Shaw. Is that you down there?'

'Max, who is it? Who's that man?'

'Can you hear me, Max? Is it you?'

Suddenly, he screamed, 'Turn off the light!'

It remained on him for several seconds more then blacked out and he felt clothed again, not stripped; felt whole again, not breaking into bits.

'Can you come up here, Max, or do you want me to come down?'

'*Who is it?*'

'Fenwick.'

A picture of the man, like light, hurt Max's tightly closed eyes. *He* had heard. That horrible man had been standing there, at the edge of the road, listening to every word.

'I think you'd better come up. It's not the place for a boy down there.'

'Max, don't you go.' Her fierce whisper was round his ankles, holding him like hands.

'There's nothing you can do there. Nothing anyone can do until daylight. And then not you. You must come up, you must answer, or I'll have to come down to get you.'

'I can't.'

'Of course you can. You'll find it considerably easier to get up than you did to get down.'

'I *can't*. Alison's here, and you blooming well know.'

'I know nothing of the kind.' (Which meant that he did; oh, yes; or he would have expressed surprise in another way.) 'Are you saying there's someone alive?'

Max peered uphill into the darkness, seething, but could see only a wall of night that lied. 'Yes, I am. She's in the truck. It's upside down. She's only fourteen. What are you pretending for? You *know*.'

'A girl, Max. Driving a truck!'

'Her Dad,' he screamed. 'Her Dad was driving it.' Then he choked up: 'Everyone's dead but her.'

Light poured again from the road, from a different point than before, probing the slope as if it were advancing a step at a time until it reached the car. For a second or two it illuminated it mercilessly.

'Max!'

'Yes.'

'I won't be long. I'll have to get a rope. It's steeper than I thought.'

Max blinked into blackness, suddenly panicked by surprise. 'Hey! Don't! You mustn't go!'

The man did not reply.

'Hey,' Max yelled, 'please, please.' He scrambled up the slope clawing for footholds and handholds, starting a torrent of stones and dirt and sticks from his feet. They beat down on to the truck striking the tray, even the cabin, clanging, and bounced on past it steeply downhill, terrifying Alison. (All boys go away; boys don't care.)

The beam of the lantern glanced back from a little farther down and picked up Max spreadeagled on the precipitous bank a few yards below the road, dirt crumbling from his feet, clinging by one hand to the sheared-off stub of a small acacia tree. Even as he forced his eyes shut against the glare, something clicked in his brain, something registered there. Innumerable marbles of cyanide, lodged like a crop of fungus puffballs.

Max heard the footsteps crunching in gravel, and from below something that must have been crying. Then the man said from above, from very close, 'Keep your mouth shut. That's cyanide. Up and out of it, boy. You give me the creeps lying there.' But the strength that should have driven Max on wouldn't come. While Alison cried he couldn't go. 'I can't reach you, Max, not without a rope, and I'm not coming down or we'll both be stuck. Dig in your heels! Push!'

'I can't.'

'Of course you can.'

'I can't leave Alison.'

'Alison won't be left. I'll look after her. I'll be back with the rope; it's no farther than the car. But your place is at home. You're needed there.'

'Why?'

'You're needed. Let it go at that. No more questions; no more talking. I said before, it's cyanide there. Do you want to die? Do you want to be poisoned? That stuff's not ashes of violets. It's sudden death.'

Max didn't move.

'Are you coming?'

'No.'

'Max, I don't want to alarm you, but it's David.'

'What about David?'

'There are lots of things about David, but I'm not going to get involved in conversation. You're not to speak another word. Dig in those heels and push!'

But Max wouldn't.

'Why *is it*, boy, at a time like this!' The voice of the man expressed an exasperation as hurtful as it was out of key. 'I want you out of there. You're making difficulties for me —as if I haven't troubles enough! I can't waste time. I'll get the rope. The car's not far.'

'You didn't worry about time, did you, or David, or anything else, when you sneaked up on Alison and me?'

But the man ignored him, the red glow of light moved off his eyelids, the footsteps crunched away. 'You're awful,' Max shrilled out of his bewilderment. 'Who do you think you are? You know what's happened here. You don't even care.'

The footsteps stopped, then came back a few paces, and Max flinched, went tight, went frightened, waiting for the light and the renewed assault of heartless words. But the light did not seek him out, the voice did not bear down, there were instead scraping sounds and the sudden tearing through foliage of an object hurled. Something struck the ground yards away and skidded, unseating dirt and stones. 'What's that?' Max yelled, but heard only stones trickling down. 'What did you do that for?' Max yelled. But the footsteps hurried away. 'What was it?' Max yelled. 'What did you throw?'

He clung to his acacia stub, still by one hand, by a single straining arm, but twisted round trying to see what the man had thrown. He was panting, he was deeply upset, but it was very dark and details were obscure; that object, that mysterious thing, could have been a canister, a broken plank, a drum, a shredded length of tyre, or any one of a dozen unidentifiable shapes.

Max whimpered a little, frustrated and hurt, and felt himself drawn back almost against his will to the anguish he shared with Alison. It was human down there with Alison, awfully hard, awfully difficult, just plain awful, but it was clean; it wasn't adult or sneaky or cruel. He'd stay with her until daylight, or noon, or night. He'd see it through until they got her out. There were others to look after David. There was no problem with David that a bolted door wouldn't solve. He'd scream, he'd kick, he'd punch, he'd throw, he'd bang his head against the wall, but then suddenly he'd forget and laugh or sleep or sing a song without words and tune.

Max let go and crabbed down on his heels and the palms of his hands, back to that one square yard of earth that was something like a sacred place.

'Alison.'

'Yes.' It was a *little* voice.

'I'm here.'

He squatted, legs crossed, hands on kneecaps, limp. 'He says he'll be back. I hope he never comes.'

'You weren't like that when you chased after him.'

'Gee, Alison.'

'Who was he?'

'Mr Fenwick.'

'Who is he to talk to you like that?'

'No one. I hardly know him.'

'Didn't seem like that to me. I thought he was your uncle or something.'

'I haven't an uncle; not here, anyway.'

'Did he throw something at you?'

'Crikey, Alison, I don't know. What would he throw anything at me for?'

'That's what I'm asking.'

He went limper still. It was such an effort. He didn't want to talk. 'It was something he picked up off the road and threw into the bush.'

'What?'

'I don't know. How should I know? Look, let's be quiet.'

'You know something, don't you? and you're not telling.'

'I don't know anything and I don't want to know. If you won't be quiet I'll sit somewhere else.'

'Thanks for not going away, Max.'

'I said I wouldn't and I won't. But that doesn't mean I won't sit somewhere else if I feel like it.'

'You're funny,' she said, 'but awfully sweet. Are all boys like you?'

He didn't answer. He was cross with her for not being quiet and suddenly not at all sure that she wasn't teasing him and might have been for half of the time. Girls were tricky. Now he could smell cyanide on his clothes and in a vague way could taste it burning like hot sand. It worried him like a pain of conscience. Perhaps it was real. Perhaps it was all in the mind.

She said, 'Give me your hand.'

But he didn't move.

'Sit closer, Max. I can't reach.'

He stirred himself. 'No. You mustn't touch.'

'Have you gone all shy or something?'

'It's cyanide.'

'I use it like salt. It's beaut with celery.'

'It's on my clothes,' he said peevishly, with open vowel sounds, 'and it's no joke. I'm stinking with the stuff.'

'Do you reckon you'll die?'

He sniffed loudly. 'I wish you'd shut up.'

Then he said, with a different voice, 'That man's coming

back. I can hear his footsteps through the ground. He's *talking* to himself.'

Every nerve of Max's body went back to the defensive. 'I won't go, Alison,' he hissed, 'I promise. He won't make me go.'

The light was up there, moving along the roadside, pouring over the edge.

'I won't go, Alison. I won't, I won't.'

The light stopped and flooded down, groping for a while, split by an intruding tree trunk. 'Max. Are you there?'

He didn't answer.

'Mrs Fenwick's here. She's come to take you back. She'll drive you down. It's important, Max, that you come. Don't make it hard for me, please.'

'I'm not going without Alison. I said before.'

The woman called. 'You're needed, Max. It's David. He's lost. If he's hiding he might answer you.'

'David's *not* lost. He's in *bed!*'

'Max, we're not here to waste time. We're here to get you. Mr Fenwick's coming down. Now be a good lad. Your loyalty is to your family. You're the man now.'

From up top there was a sudden scramble, a shower of pebbles and stones, and the limbs and body of a man floundering in the cone of light, and a thudding on the hill like a heavy-footed animal. He slipped and skidded, frantically trying to arrest the speed of his descent. 'Frank,' the woman cried. He crashed against a tree with a grunt of violently expelled air, and dropped from the knees, drooped and clung there.

'*Frank!*' The quality of alarm in the woman's voice turned her cry into a shriek that came to Max as a surprise. Who could possibly care what happened to a man like that? Even though he clung there like something whole at the bottom and top but broken in the middle? Even though the force of the blow hurt in the pit of Max's own stomach and became a shout, 'Mr Fenwick! What have you done?'

Alison cried, 'What has he done?'

Mrs Fenwick shrieked, 'Are you all right?'

He weakly waved an arm as though throwing something away, and groaned, 'My God; what a hill.'

'Are you all right, Frank?' It was the fourth call from higher up, this time answered; 'Yes, yes.' Then he came hobbling across, almost on his knees, using his hands, obviously forcing himself to move. 'Is that where the girl is?' he gasped. 'In there?'

'Yes,' Max said. 'In here.'

The lantern beam from the road moved with him, a foot or two above him, with shadows and glare and sparkling glances on frosted foliage. He was muttering and steadied himself against the cabin, leaning. 'My God, what a mess. Is she hurt?'

'No.'

'She should be dead. Luck of the devil.' He was ghastly white but that could not be seen. 'And her name's Alison McPhee.' It came out quietly, in an undertone.

'Did I say that?'

'You didn't. But McPhee's the name on the door.' He pushed himself away from it, swaying, and glanced up the hill towards the source of the light. To Max the glance meant nothing, to Frank Fenwick it was part of an inner tension that was almost past bearing. He had thrown McPhee's sign into the scrub, hidden his motives, lied, done everything within the power of a man to conceal a truth from his wife where it was everywhere apparent. There she stood, a huge white eye creating the light she needed to see by, yet not knowing what she saw. Not knowing; and by the grace of God she would never guess.

Then he sighed. 'Max. Just look. Rope everywhere.'

'Eh?'

'Scrag ends of it, boy, by the yard. Why didn't you tell me there was rope all over the place? Why make me run to the car? Why make me bring my wife back? I didn't want her here.'

'I didn't make you do anything,' Max shrilled. 'I didn't know there was rope on the truck. I can't see in the dark.' As he spoke, he became aware of light. The awareness of light was an awareness of Alison; an almost frightening compulsion to drop to his knees to peer into the wreck, at the same time a wild urge to run away. But there was a hand on his arm, allowing neither one thing nor the other. 'What have you kids been up to?' The voice was stern, paternal, self-possessed.

'That's none of your business.'

'Isn't it? You might be surprised. But don't let's bog down again, young fellow. Let me tell you you're playing with fire. Enough's enough. Let's wind it up. You're needed at home. I'll attend to things here.'

Blood rushed to Max's head but the pressure of the hand on his arm tightened suddenly and changed his protest to a gasp of hurt.

'I don't want to get rough, Max, but I feel strongly about this, and my body's a good deal tougher than yours. Go home. Do as you're told.'

'Who are you to order me around?'

'The one useful friend you've got in the world at this moment.'

Alison's cry seemed to come up out of the earth. 'Don't listen to him, Max. You promised to stay.'

'So you're there, are you? I was wondering when we'd hear. It's a promise he'll be breaking, my dear. Max is the man in his family and his family needs him. His little brother ran away, out through the door, and his little brother is mentally retarded, or didn't he say? Max will take care of his brother and I'll take care of you.'

'I want Max to take care of me . . .'

'That's not the way we'll have it.'

Max said, in a dull, tired voice, 'How did David get out?'

Audibly, the man breathed heavily through his nose. 'From a miscalculation. In a rash moment I broke down the door. I'm sorry. But feeling sorry about it is a waste of time. We've been looking for hours. It's very dangerous here for a little boy whose logic is different from yours or mine.'

'Max, don't listen to him!'

But Max, inside, was turning into dreary greys, into a feeling like mists and cold. (Mum used to say: 'David comes first. Last in all things, but first.') 'Why didn't you tell me up there?' he sighed. 'Why didn't you tell me before? Why wait until now?'

Frank Fenwick had no answer, no honest answer, no ready and immediate lie. He had not thought of it then, up there.

But Alison cried, 'You wouldn't, Max. You couldn't. You're not to go.'

'Brenda and Tony need you, boy. They've had a hard time. And it's a man's job here. You know that. So do I.'

The woman called from the road, 'Hurry along, there.'

Alison shrilled, 'Don't listen to them. *It's not fair.* I want to see you, you know how much. I want you to be here when I get out.'

But Max, wearily, had made up his mind. 'I'll come back,' he said, 'as soon as I can. It's David, Alison. He's such a little boy.'

'You're not to come back! You're to stay away!'

'I can't stay away, Mr Fenwick. You don't understand.'

'It's no place for you, that's all I understand.' The strength of the man began to bear with direct and guiding force against Max's arm, and Max went with him, not resisting.

'Max! You mustn't!'

He tried to say goodbye to her, and in a way he did, but the words wouldn't form for anyone to hear. He went with the man like a dumb animal on a lead, up the hill, leaving the wreckage behind. 'I'm coming,' he said, 'you don't need to force me.'

'I'm not forcing you, Max, but I've got to make sure. And when you get home change those clothes. You stink, boy, of cyanide and oil.'

'Max,' Alison cried. 'Please, please. I'll never see you again if you go. You can't go like this. You *promised* to stay.'

If ever he smelt cyanide again he'd think of Alison. Whenever he smelt oil he'd think of her. Whenever there was a fog or noises in the night. Every time he travelled by train on the line that went out to St Clare's, the wrong St Clare's, the wrong city.

The lantern beam streamed above his head. He stumbled

into the glare with the man's hand on his arm and didn't even see Dad's car.

'The rope's firm,' Frank Fenwick said, 'tied to a sapling at the top. It'll help you up the bank. Take a good grip on it. Up you go.'

Someone else was reaching down. 'Come on, Max. Give me your hand.'

He was sitting on the road.

'The poor kid's in a daze. What a wonderful boy he's been.'

'Toss the torch, Phyllis. You'll find your way all right. If you can manage it, when you've fixed the kids, bring back the car. I'll have to go through to Hamer, probably with the girl, and for police and ambulances and the rest. We're going to need some strong-nerved men to gather this cyanide up before it rains. Be quick, Phyllis.'

'*Max!*' Alison's cry was far away.

'It'll mean your walking to the shacks, Phyllis, later on. You'll have to get back there; we can't leave these kids alone. You'll have to walk, I'm afraid. There's no other way. Do you mind?'

'I don't mind. . . . Come on, Max. The car's not far.'

He heard as though life was lived outside and he was in a room. Now it was for the man to skid down the hill and occupy the sacred square yard.

'*Max!*'

But Max didn't answer. He wasn't there.

'What are you doing to that boy?' It was a voice she didn't want to hear. 'Leave him alone.'

'You horrible man,' Alison cried. 'You don't understand.'

'I think I might. How old did you say you were?'

'That's nothing to do with you.' Then she yelled, '*Max!*'

'For heaven's sake!' He banged his fist on the side of the cabin. 'Stop it at once. Whine, whine, whine.'

'That's not fair!'

'It seems perfectly fair to me.'

'You haven't been here; you don't understand.'

'I understand considerably more than you suppose. I

was coping with young women of your age before you were born. Now behave yourself, and be satisfied you're alive.'

'Oh, leave me alone.'

He bent low and flashed the light inside, but she had turned her back and he saw only her hair. He shuddered a little but the voice was firm, 'Chin up, Alison. I want you to get used to the idea that I *am* on your side.'

'Get lost . . .'

'You'll be in trouble if I do.' He held the lantern light almost with affection on her hair. 'You've got spirit girl. I like your style.'

'No one would ever guess!'

'When you're a little older and a little wiser, you'll know. You've an awful lot to learn, my dear.'

'I'm not your dear.'

He smiled. 'I suppose not.' But inwardly he thought, 'How do I wriggle out of this? The world, suddenly, seems very small. So big for so long; now so small. Phyllis will hear of it or read it or Max will blab it for sure, if she hasn't already guessed. Alison, it'd be Heaven for a week but Hell for evermore. Do we take our Heaven and pay our Hell?'

He went down on one knee. 'Where's your mother?' he said aloud. 'How do I get in touch with her?'

She didn't answer.

'She'll have to be told. When there's an accident these things have got to be done quickly.'

'I haven't a mother.'

'You must have, lass, somewhere or other. If she's not dead. And she's not, is she? She's very much alive.'

'She's not dead.'

'You know that you're going to need her now.'

'Oh, go away. I don't know who my mother is.'

'Your father was on his own? Is that it?'

'I don't know what you mean.'

'I mean was he married to anyone else? Have you a stepmother?'

'No,' she said sullenly, 'Dad had friends. What are you asking all these questions for?'

'What was your father doing on this road?'

'I'm not answering your questions. Go away.'

Silently, Frank Fenwick asked the question of himself: 'What did he bring you here for? At night, on this road? He must have been mad, or didn't the poor devil know? Of course he knew. Did he plan it or was it impulse? Either way it's still mad. All brawn, no brains—Phyllis's words— but not necessarily true. Ten years is a long time and he's not been near us before. He's played the game by Phyllis and me; he was a good man.'

'Alison, I've got to put it to you again. Why was your father on this road?'

'I don't know.'

'Of course you know.'

'I said I don't.'

Had McPhee suddenly made up his mind and got caught by circumstances he couldn't control? Once on the road, by night in a fog, he'd never have been able to turn; he'd have had to come through. Impulse or chance or deliberate design? Had she been asking questions about her mother, wanting to meet her, or did he think it was time?

'Please, Alison.'

'You're so persistent,' she sighed. 'You won't believe what I say.'

'I'll be the judge of that.'

'Fred Finn,' she said, 'it was because of him. He was going to stop at Fred's place because of the fog. But you've never heard of him, so what difference does it make?'

'No. I've never heard of him.'

'I told you so.'

'Told me what?'

'That you wouldn't believe me. Max didn't either. Twenty-three miles, Dad said, from the turn-off, to Finn's Folly. You might say, Mr Fenwick, it didn't work out.'

Then she felt surprised and churned-up. Words that had been going somewhere suddenly came to a stop. His silence was different from before, not the silence of frustration or of nothing to say, but of something held back. 'Well?' Alison said.

She heard a sound she had heard before, heavy breathing through the nose. 'I don't know, Alison. But did your father mistake the distance as he mistook the name! At *thirty*-three miles there's a place called Phyll's Folly.' He didn't want to say it but it came. 'There was an article about it a while ago in a TV magazine. They got the distance right but the name wrong.'

'They called it Finn's Folly?'

'Yes, my dear. They did.'

She turned over inch by inch until her face came into the light, a hard light that the man directed to one side until it softened. There were bruises and dirt and oil and smudges where Max had placed his hand. She was a surprisingly ordinary little girl.

'Who's lying to me?' she asked. 'Dad, or Max, or you?'

'I'll get you out of there. Then we'll see.'

'I want to know now.'

'There's no simple answer, Alison.'

'*Phyll* has something to do with Mrs Fenwick, hasn't it? Is that why Dad was so nervous and strange?'

'Sometimes, Alison, when you start things off you get frightened of where they might go. It happened to your father and it's happening to me. Dead men don't answer for what they leave behind, but living men do. Your mother's not far away Alison. She's very near.'

Phyllis Fenwick, feeling her way, walked slowly with Max into darkness made more intense because the light had gone. His feet dragged and his weight was heavy on her arm. Then his weight became stubborn and wouldn't move. 'Come on, Max; it's over now.'

'Blow David,' he said, 'getting lost. I wanted to stay. I promised to stay.'

'Was staying so desperately important, Max?'

Everything that held him together was breaking apart. 'Alison's a pretty name.'

'Yes, it is.'

'St Clare's in Adelaide. That's where she goes. You'd have thought it would have been Melbourne, wouldn't you?'

'Alison McPhee, I suppose?'

'She's lost her Dad; isn't it a shame?'

'He was a good Dad, I'm sure.'

'She hated herself for the things she said to him.'

'I understand what she means.'

'I've lost my Dad, too, and my Mum. Do you reckon it's fair?'

'One day, Max, it happens to us all.'

'Yeh, yeh; but not to Mum and Dad.'

'For some it comes early; for some it comes late; the clock doesn't care.'

'Alison hasn't a Mum either.'

'Is that what she said?'

'Her Mum went away. Could you imagine any Mum going away from a girl like her?'

'Things happen to people, Max, sometimes difficult for others to understand.'

'But for her mother to go away . . .'

'It was bad. It was bad. And it's harder now.'

'I haven't even seen her. I'm tired.'

She held him by the waist and held on hard. 'It's all over, Max. You met her one night; you went away. You'll meet a hundred more like her, you'll see.'

'That's not fair.'

'And sometimes they'll go away from you. Come on, Max. Come along. The car's not far.'

'You're *cruel*.'

'Perhaps. But for the men I love I know what's best.'

'You don't love me!'

'You're not a man.'

He went with her, drawn along. She was strong and determined that he should move, but he felt a thousand miles from her. He couldn't understand the workings of her mind, the things she said were cruel. Then he saw the parking lights of the car, misted by fog.

'How are you going to get down?' he said.

'I'll back until I can turn.'

'There's nowhere to turn.'

'That's my worry, Max, not yours. It won't be the first

time I've turned on this road. It's a small car.' Her grip tightened. 'There are people waiting here; you're not to run away. These are the people who need you. Alison is in very good hands.'

Something warned him; something got through to the Max who had been led away from the sacred square yard. Something like nerves or energy or prickling distrust swept through him from head to toe, and she felt it, she knew. Her hand tightened until it pinched his arm. 'No, Max,' she said, 'I intend Mr Fenwick to handle that situation alone, to decide for himself and for me. It's no place for you now, up there.'

He tried to disengage his arm, troubled more and more by the incongruity of her words, but she quickened her stride and bore him on with her momentum to the car.

She opened the front passenger door for him and the courtesy light showed them inside, huddled in the back: Brenda, as bedraggled as she had ever been, nursing David possessively; David asleep, David like someone who had been roughed up in a brawl; and Tony, Tony with circles for eyes, staring.

This was his family. They were real.

Phyllis Fenwick released his arm. 'Max? Are you a man?'

He didn't know that her hand had gone.

'Hi, Brenda. Hi, Tortoise.'

Brenda smiled and without words acknowledged that something had changed.

Tony said, 'Gee, Max, I'm glad you're here.'

Then he sat in the car and after a little while sighed. 'First job I guess, is to turn that cranky old engine over back at the shack and recharge the batteries for some power.'

About the Author

Ivan Southall was born in 1921. He was sixteen when his first article was accepted by the Melbourne *Herald*. He then wrote some thirty stories and articles which were published all over Australia. Ivan Southall served with the R.A.A.F. for five and a half years during the Second World War, beginning operational flights from Britain in 1943. He was awarded the D.F.C. in 1944. In 1945 he was posted to the War History Section of the R.A.A.F. Overseas Headquarters, London, to write a portion of the history of the R.A.A.F.

Ivan Southall has since become well known, both in his own country and overseas, for his biography of the Australian war hero, Bluey Truscott, his account of the exploits of Australian mine disposal officers in Britain during the war, *Softly Tread the Brave*, and for his many award-winning children's books.

He now lives in the Dandenong Ranges, near Melbourne, and concentrates on writing for young readers. He says he 'enjoys writing for children more than any other activity'.

*Another book by Ivan Southall,
available in a Puffin edition, is
described on the following page*

Bread and Honey

Anzac Day was never just an ordinary holiday
without school in Michael Cameron's house.
Grandma was always up late the night before
making a wreath of chrysanthemums – green
for ten million heroes, white for sorrows,
red for love – to place at the foot of the War
Memorial in Main Street, after the sound of
drums and marching men and medals jingling
had died away.

For 13-year-old Michael, unsure of himself,
lonely since his troubles with the Farlows
who lived next door, confused by the conflicts
in his own family and in the world about him,
this particular Anzac morning is to prove
more important than any other he has known,
even though he misses the parade, and only
hears the drums and trumpets in
the distance.

Because of his meeting with Margaret,
on the rain-swept seashore beyond the tea-tree
scrub, and his subsequent dramatic encounter
with Bully Boy MacBaren and Flackie, the
bully's hanger-on, Michael finds, quite
suddenly, that some of his confusion is resolved,
that he can begin to look for his own answers
to the problems and the conflict
in his world.

For readers of eleven and over.